for joining!
XOXO
Laramie
Briscoe

CUTTER

LAUREL SPRINGS EMERGENCY RESPONSE TEAM #4

LARAMIE BRISCOE

Editor: Elfwerks Editing

Beta Readers: Danielle Wentworth

Proofreader: Danielle Wentworth

Cover: Laramie Briscoe

Cover Photography: Wander Aguiar

Formatting: Laramie Briscoe

 Created with Vellum

ALSO BY LARAMIE BRISCOE

Heaven Hill Shorts

Caelin

Christine

Justice

Harley

Jagger

Charity

Liam

Drew

Dalton

Mandy

Rockin' Country Series

Only The Beginning

One Day at A Time

The Price of Love

Full Circle

Hard To Love

Reaper's Girl

The Nashvegas Trilogy

Power Couple

The Moonshine Task Force Series

Renegade

Tank

Havoc

Ace

Menace

Cruise

Laurel Springs Emergency Response Team

Ransom

Suppression

Enigma

Cutter

Sullivan

The MVP Duet

On the DL

MVP

The Midnight Cove Series

Inflame

Stand Alones

Sketch

Sass

Trick

Room 143

2018 Laramie Briscoe Compilation

2019 Laramie Briscoe Compilation

NEW RELEASE ALERTS

JOIN MY MAILING LIST

http://sitel.ink/LBList

JOIN MY READERS GROUP

fbl.ink/LaramiesLounge

MOONSHINE TASK FORCE MEMBERS

Ryan "Renegade" Kepler – Married to Whitney and father to Stella and Nick. Best friend to Trevor.

Trevor "Tank" Trumboldt – Married to Blaze, brother to Whitney, uncle to Stella and Nick. Best friend to Ryan.

Holden "Havoc" Thompson – Married to Leighton, father to Ransom and Cutter. Best friend to Mason.

Anthony "Ace" Bailey – Married to Violet.

Mason "Menace" Harrison – Married to Karina, father to Caleb and Kelsea, grandfather to Molly and Levi. Best friend to Holden.

Caleb "Cruise" Harrison – Married to Ruby, father to Molly and Levi, son of Mason, brother to Kelsea.

BLURB

Cutter Thompson

Hurricane Tatum, a category five storm hell-bent on making landfall along the Alabama coast, is my opportunity to show my friends and family the kind of man I've become.

The kid who lost his scholarship and the love is life is ready for a change. A change I'm equal parts scared will and won't come.

An EMT wasn't my first choice of careers, but it's become my calling. When the winds die down, the skies clear, and the rain stops, we're left with devastation the likes of I've never seen.

What I come to realize is ugly destruction can be beautiful, if we can only figure out what perspective to see it.

Rowan Baker

The LSERT is a Godsend, especially as us local first responders emerge from our shelters to see our town and homes destroyed. It's going to take time to rebuild.

Rebuilding is what I'm used to. After I watched my four-year-old daughter die in my arms I've done nothing but try to find a reason to live.

But I've got baggage. Memories, an ex-husband, and a fear I won't be able to save everyone.

When I meet Cutter Thompson, he reminds me rebuilding can mean letting go of fear and allowing myself to live the life I've wanted all along.

PROLOGUE

Cutter

"DIDN'T EVEN SHAVE?"

I roll my eyes as Tucker and Major walk toward me. Karsyn follows closely behind, not because she's coming with us, but because she wants to see her boys off. At least that's what Tucker told me when I texted him, asking if he wanted a ride this morning.

"Something tells me a beard and my tattoos are going to be the least of anyone's worries over the next few weeks."

Reaching down, I give Major a few scratches, watching as the rest of the crew heading down to the Gulf coast show up.

"You've definitely got a point there." Karsyn hugs her arms tightly to her body.

It's not necessarily cold, but it is three in the morning. "Are you going to meet us down there? If we have to stay longer than a few weeks?"

She nods. "Depends on what's happening here. There

are a lot of you going down. We can't have a shortage in Laurel Springs and still expect to help people who need it."

"Makes sense."

Tucker reaches back, grabbing hold of her hand. This is my cue to leave them alone. Looking out over everyone who has gathered here, I spot a few members of my family.

"Hey, Dad." I walk up to him, enveloping the larger-than-life man I've idolized since childhood, in a huge hug.

He pats me on the back.

"You doin' good?"

We separate. I nod, sticking my hands in my jeans pockets. "Could be worse. Slightly nervous."

"This is your first time being sent somewhere else to help, it's normal to be nervous. I'm nervous for you. Be sure and do what they ask of you, and please be smart."

The words he uses make my skin crawl. I know he doesn't mean them the way I'm taking them. It's hard though, to not take them in a negative connotation, after the shit I've pulled in my life.

"I promise, I'll make you proud."

His green eyes flash with a spark of hurt. "You already made me proud, Cutter. Don't think you haven't. I just know you haven't been in a situation like this before, and I want you to be safe."

"Yeah, fucker." I hear Ransom, and I have to smirk. "Be safe out there."

I turn to where Ransom has come up behind me, Rambo with him, and Keegan holding his hand. "Why the hell is he awake at three a.m.?" I point down to my nephew.

"I've learned not to question it, and he asked to see you before you left. Since Momma's at work, we're bending the rules, right?" He looks down at Keegan.

He zips his mouth and throws away the key.

"Nice," I chuckle, bending down to pick him up. "I'm gonna miss you, my man."

He hugs me tightly around the neck. "You gonna miss me?"

"Mmm hmmm." He nods, grabbing hold of my neck. He leans in, kissing me on the nose. It's one of the cutest things he's ever done. "When I get back, we'll go for ice cream. Cool?"

"Yes!"

He can't speak many words yet, but he sure can understand what others are saying to him. He's smart as hell, so much smarter than me. "Love you." I hug him tightly.

"Love you, too."

Putting him down on the ground, I glance at Dad. "Mom too worried to come?"

He nods. "You know how she is."

"She does realize I'm an EMT, right? It's not like I'm a cop." I hit Ransom in the stomach.

He doubles over, coughing.

Dad shakes his head. "She knows. She sends her love and says to be careful. Text and call her every day. Text and call, Cutter."

"I got it, you all act like I'm a teenager going away for college. I am in my mid-twenties. I can handle myself."

"But you'll always be my kid brother." Ransom grabs me around the neck. "For real, be safe." His voice takes on a serious tone.

"I will," I say, my tone serious too.

"Leaving in five minutes!" Someone yells.

"I'm gonna get going. Tucker and me are driving down together."

Dad holds his arms open. "You do what Tucker tells you to do. If they tell you to put a vest on, you put it on. When things like this happen, there can and will be tremendous violence if people get desperate."

"I know." I hug him tightly. "I'll be fine. Text and call," I chuckle.

"You better include me on that text," he gruffly answers.

"Me too, go ahead and add Stelle. She won't forgive me if you don't keep in touch while you're gone."

"Maybe I want your ass to be in the doghouse."

"Love you too, bro." He grins.

I throw him a wave, before bending down to give Keegan another hug. With that, I grab my bag, holding it over my shoulder. Tucker is waiting for me with Major.

"You ready?"

"As ready as I'll ever be." I sigh as I look around at all the people saying goodbye to family and friends. Even though I'm worried and slightly scared, I'm proud to be part of this first wave going down to help in the wake of what everyone thinks will be a historic hurricane.

Tucker and I secure the provisions we're taking with us and get Major situated in the back cab of the truck before the two of us get inside. We're toward the back of the caravan, and when we finally get going, my heart is pounding.

Not because I'm terrified this is going to change my life.

Because I'm terrified it won't.

CHAPTER ONE

Cutter

"HAVE YOU EVER BEEN IN A HURRICANE?"

Tucker looks over at me. We're in a hotel, about ten miles inland. Close enough to help, but far enough away to be safe from the storm surge. The Weather Channel has been on non-stop, and I'm starting to recognize the names on the screen. One thing I am sure of? If Jim Cantore is where you are, shit's about to get real. Jim Cantore is ten miles from where we are.

To say I'm nervous would be an understatement, but those of us in roles like myself and Tucker's are in aren't supposed to show it. Instead we're expected to sit in this small hotel room, with our two queen beds, and pretend it doesn't feel like the world's about to end. Already, I'm beginning to think about what it's going to look like once the storm passes, how many people are we going to help. What will the situation be like as far as what access we'll have to materials?

"I was in Katrina." He rubs at Major's head slowly. He drops this bomb like it's nothing.

"No shit?" The admission surprises me. I've never heard this before.

"Yup, I was in New Orleans at the time. Fifteen years old and the most disobedient fuck you've ever seen in your life. I had older friends and they all wanted to hit up a party place before school started that year. Back then school didn't start until after Labor Day, so we were like we'll go for the weekend, come back, and our parents won't know."

"Did you not realize a hurricane was coming?"

He chuckles. "I'm sure we knew one was coming, because it was all over the news, but I don't think we realized the possible impact of a storm that size. We found out real quick."

"Were you in New Orleans when it hit?"

"Yeah, smack dab in the middle. We didn't have enough money for a hotel, so we were sleeping in my buddy's Tahoe. When we realized what was happening, we went to the lobby of a hotel. There were police there and we explained the situation to them. Luckily for us, the hotel allowed us to stay in the lobby. If it hadn't been for them, we would have died. As it was, we had to take higher ground and get rescued by the Coast Guard. I got my ass beat when I got home. I mean beat, but I didn't even care because I was so happy to be alive, it just didn't matter."

"Nothing is ever easy with you, is it?"

He grins. "Never."

"Well now I feel a little better, knowing you've been through hell and survived," I tease.

"It was worse than what I imagine hell would be like. We were stuck there for days without water. It was awful, and I don't wish it on my worst enemy. The sound is something I'll never forget, then the rising water. It literally would not stop. We're lucky, luckier than we had a right to be." He takes a drink of the water beside him. "I was grounded for a year when I got home, but I learned a great respect for Mother Nature and God himself. I don't think I ever prayed that much in my life before. I didn't think I was going to make it. If there's anything that'll get you closer to God, it's a natural disaster."

"Do you think this will be as bad?"

I'm watching the weatherman on TV, and he's warning anyone who will listen about storm surge, winds, rain, tornados, and the possibility of flooding well inland. There's also the threat of power outages and no clean water. It's all very ominous and I realize quickly how lucky I am to have a home that will still be there when I head back up north. I don't have to worry about electricity and water. Nor do I have to worry about any of my family being lost in the immediate aftermath of the storm.

"I don't know." Tucker rubs a hand over his face. "This one is plenty big, and the water temp is high. It looks like it's going to be bad." He shrugs. "But I'm not God or a psychic and I can't tell the future. We'll do what we can to brace for impact and then we'll work on getting these people the help they need. That's all we can do."

I wish I was as confident as Tucker. It's almost as if nothing shakes or spooks him. I know it does, but he doesn't show it.

The noise of the TV in the background reminds me of why we're here in the first place.

Hurricane Tatum is churning in the gulf, taking aim at the coast. Those of you in Gulf Shores and Orange Beach are under mandatory evacuation. We are looking at a landfall somewhere over the next twelve hours. Outer rain bands are already making their presence known. Mobile, watch out for storm surge in the bay. Flooding will be a major impact of this storm. Right now, Tatum is at a Cat 4, and the waters are warm. We're predicting she'll intensify into a Cat 5 before she makes landfall. The time for preparation is over. You've either evacuated or you'll need to shelter in place. Please be aware that rescue may not be possible.

"Why wouldn't you evacuate?" I whisper as I watch the huge storm on TV.

"Some people can't afford it." He nods to Major. "Some people have dogs that are more family than pet and they aren't allowed to take them into shelters. After Katrina that was supposed to have been stopped, but I've heard of people being turned away with a pet, so they stay. Others are scared to leave their homes because they're afraid they'll never see them again. There are numerous reasons."

I look over at Tucker, my eyes wide open. "I guess you're right. I never thought about it that way."

"It's cool, you haven't had a ton of life experience yet. Once you've dealt with a few disasters, you'll be able to figure out when you need to panic, and when you don't. More often than not, I try to temper my reactions. The quicker I react, the worse I seem to take it. It's important to give it the attention it needs, but not to let it overtake your entire life. You'll learn."

The sigh that comes from my throat is more frustrated than bored. "Everybody says that." I flop back on the bed. "When am I going to stop being the guy who lost his scholarship and came back home with his tail tucked between his legs?"

"When you stop letting that shit define you, Cutter. You're so much more than that, but until you start seeing yourself differently, no one else is going to see you differently."

I think about what he says. "It was the biggest failure of my life," my voice is soft as I admit what many perceive as my shame. "To know I had everything right here." I hold out my hand, my palm facing upward. "And I fucked it up."

"That's one of the best things you can do, admit you made a mistake. You can come back from it, Cutter. At some point, if you keep showing up, people will realize you're showing up."

"I just always feel like I'm compared to Ransom." I run a hand through my hair. "Wife, kid, dog, I fuckin' can't even compete with that. Can't even keep a damn plant alive, much less a pet or another human being."

"You really think that?" Tucker looks over at me, his eyebrows scrunched together. The disbelief in his voice surprises me. "You think people compare you to Ransom?"

"Oh, I know they do."

I can distinctly remember when Stelle and Ransom got married. Mom pulled me aside and said something along the lines of you can only hope to find a woman like this. Which brought back all the memories of what happened.

"No, they don't," Tucker argues. "If anything, people admire you."

"That's bullshit. You and I both know it."

"It's not bullshit. You've overcome a lot, my man. Most people would have put their head in the sand and never lifted it out after what happened to you. It took a lot of heart and determination to become the man you are now. You didn't let it make you bitter, but you have to make sure to forgive yourself for it, Cutter. You didn't know."

Now I'm interested in how he knows. "What do you mean I didn't know? Has someone talked to you about what happened to me?"

Tucker's face drains of color, and I know someone has. "Ransom and I spend a lot of time together."

"Don't defend him." I sit up, swinging my feet over the side of the bed. "That wasn't his story to tell."

"Sometimes the ones you think aren't affected, are. Maybe he had issues with what happened to you, Cutter. Maybe he felt like it was partially his fault. Did you ever think he feels partially responsible?"

"How? Why?" This makes no sense to me. What happened to me, happened to *me*, no one else.

"Those are questions you should ask your brother, but I promise you, you aren't in this alone. You never were."

I'm not sure I want to know the answer to those questions. My mind is swirling as I lie back against the pillows. I want nothing more than to sleep, but as I hear the wind picking up outside, I know sleep won't come. This may very well be the longest night of my life.

The storm coming ashore doesn't compare to the one I have raging inside my head and my heart.

CHAPTER TWO

Rowan

DEVASTATION.

I've felt it before. You don't bury your four-year-old daughter and not feel it. But this? This is destruction.

"Isn't that where *The Juke Box* used to be?"

I nod, listening to my brother, Sullivan, list off places that used to be on Main Street in our small town of Paradise Lost, Alabama. Everywhere the eye can see, there's debris and water. So much water.

I'm standing in ankle-deep sludge as we speak. The rain is still coming down, but not as hard as it was hours ago. Thank God for rain boots; without them, I'd probably be risking some sort of waterborne illness no one has discovered yet.

"Should we start going door-to-door?"

He looks down at me, a harsh look on his face. "First of all, little sister of mine, I'm the police, you're an EMT. If anybody will start going door-to-door before this storm's over, it's gonna be me. Second of all, we haven't been given the go ahead. Honestly, we should still be sheltering."

I know he speaks the truth, but I can't stand to be waiting.

Waiting to see what's going to happen.

The same way I waited for my daughter to die.

I'm a woman of action, and this goes against every single part of who I've become since that awful day.

"Does that mean I have to get back inside?" I point to the fire station I've been staged at.

"I could arrest you if you don't." He gives me a grin.

"I'd fight you."

"Resisting arrest," he laughs. "Keep adding charges."

I roll my eyes dramatically. "You're a pain in my ass."

"You're a pain in my whole body," he retorts. "But get in there. We still got a few hours of this shit to go. I'll be back to check on y'all later."

"Be safe." I reach over to wrap my arms around him.

"You too, if you need anything, you know how to get hold of me."

Slowly, I walk back over to the fire station, not wanting to go back in. Since the incident, I've always wanted to see things coming at me head on. If there's a storm, I'm outside watching it. If I go to the doctor, I ask them not to ease into any bad news. I want to know. If I can see it coming, I can prepare.

Surprises?

Those are the things that I can't prepare for, and they're my biggest fear.

I get to the door, but before I walk in, I look back out at the street, seeing Sullivan with his neon vest. Reaching down, I grab the necklace I always wear. Lifting it up to my lips, I kiss the metal circle.

In my mind, I say my wish. *Etta, please keep Uncle Sullivan safe. Love you!*

She'll never hear me say those words again, but I think them a hundred thousand times throughout the day.

"How bad is it?"

My partner, Isaac, didn't want to see the destruction, not yet. He's the type who has to prepare himself. I'm the realist, he's the optimist.

"Bad," I answer. "There's only two buildings standing on this street, and we're obviously in one of them. The water has done a lot of damage too."

Luckily the fire station is on a hill and has been spared most of the flooding, but we still have high tide to go, and we're out of sandbags.

He sighs. "I guess we should go watch the weather."

I groan. We've done nothing but watch the weather for over a week. Ever since this storm became one to keep ann eye on. "I'd much rather be out helping people."

"Same, but we're supposed to wait for the okay."

Meaning we have to wait for the governor to tell us it's okay to leave our shelter. The only people allowed out now are military and police.

"It'll be our time to shine soon." He rubs at the back of my neck.

How do I explain it's not even about shining? I don't do my job for the thank you; I do it for the victims who needed help and didn't get it.

Instead of answering him, I walk over to the cot that's been designated mine and take a seat. If I have to wait, I might as well try to get some rest. As soon as we're released, the work will be non-stop.

THE SOUND of an alarm wakes me up. I'm groggy, trying to find my balance as I push myself up from the cot. My mouth almost refuses to work as I try to get words out. "Are we clear?" I shout out, I don't know who I'm asking, but I'm hoping someone answers.

"We're clear." I hear Isaac's voice behind me. "And we've got a scene to get to."

He puts something in my hands. Immediately I know they're my glasses. "Thank you!"

"I know how you are when you first wake up. Put 'em on and get yourself situated. A building has collapsed, and there's a lot of injured."

Immediately I feel my adrenaline spike.

This is what I live for. The satisfaction of helping someone. Of knowing in their darkest hour, I can save them.

Because I couldn't save *her*.

Instead I save *them*.

We run to our ambulance, along with the firefighters sprinting to their engines.

"Follow us!" They shout. "The water is still high; we'll make way for you."

My heart pounds as the bay doors open and we tuck in behind the first engine. They weren't wrong. The water is flood-worthy, but we have to do what we have to do. I'm hanging onto the handle over the door.

"Whatever you do, don't stop pressing the gas." I lift my feet up as some water seeps into the sides of the ambulance.

"I got this." Isaac grips the wheel, holding it steady, breathing easier as we head further inland.

The water still surrounds us, but not nearly as much as we were just in.

Once we break free, he slams the pedal to the floor, following behind, as we make our way to the building.

I try not to look at what's surrounding us, but I can't help it. Many places of my hometown are no longer standing. I want nothing more than to check on my parents, but last time I pulled my phone out, I had no service. Who knows when that'll come back online.

"Do you think it'd be bad if I radioed dispatch to see if they can get info on my parents?"

"I was about to ask the same question to you," Isaac laughs. "I want to make sure Britt and Justin are okay." He mentions his wife and son. "I know they bunkered down at my in-laws and they should be fine, but I'd really like to know."

"We'll wait and see if someone else does it first."

Nobody wants to be the first one to ask a favor like that when there are definitely casualties and lots of people now without a home.

"Shit, there's a lot of debris up here." He whistles as he slows the ambulance down substantially.

We're picking our way through pieces of trees, homes, and who knows what else as we try to get to the collapse that called for paramedics. When it comes to a stop, one of the firefighters comes back to us. "We've got a large tree blocking the road. We're gonna need to cut it before we can get through."

Again, waiting is something I can't do.

Unbuckling, I get out of the ambulance, going around to

the back.

"What are you doing?" Isaac yells. "Ro, what the fuck?"

I've grabbed a go bag and gotten what I can carefully fit in it.

"I can't wait around here knowing there are people who need our help. You stay with the rig and I'll go on. I don't mind walking."

"I'm not letting you go alone," he argues.

"That's cool." A deep voice says behind me. "I'll go with her."

Turning, I see someone I don't know. But he wears an EMT uniform that signifies he's part of the Laurel Springs Emergency Response Team. We'd heard they'd be coming to help us.

"My partner, Tucker, is waiting with our caravan. A few of us are walking ahead to triage. She's okay with us." He gestures to a group of men, and a few women. "We'll make sure she's okay."

This man. He's nothing like I've ever seen before. Tattooed, sure of himself, tall, and strong.

"See, I'll be fine."

Even if I'm not, I know how to take care of myself.

Isaac nods. "See you when I get there."

"Don't take too long," I joke.

"Let's go," I tell the guy who offered to walk with me.

"After you." He gestures ahead with his hand.

"Thank you for offering to go with me, he wouldn't have let me go. We've been partners since we started, and he's super protective. Like an older brother, of which I already have two."

"No problem, I'm a younger sibling too, so I understand how it goes."

“So annoying.” I shake my head.

He puts his hand on my arm, effectively stopping us. “I’m Cutter, just in case you need me later.”

“Rowan.” I don’t add a caveat. Something tells me, almost every woman Cutter comes into contact with needs him later.

And me? Well I’m just not that kind of girl.

But fate? It has a really funny way of pushing us where we need to go, not where we want to.

CHAPTER THREE

Cutter

THIS WOMAN BESIDE ME, walking into what could equate to the belly of the beast, doesn't look like she's prepared for it. Rowan, such a regal name for such a small lady. Glasses cover her hazel eyes. Dark hair is up in some sort of knot on top of her head. She barely comes to my collarbone, doesn't look like she weighs much either, I could probably pick her up and put her over my shoulder.

Not that I'm going to do it, but I'm trying to make a point.

The silence, it's killing me.

"Are you from here?" I ask as we trudge through sticks, leaves, and who knows what else.

"Born and raised," she answers. "First situation I've ever been through like this, though. You?"

"I came down from Laurel Springs with the LSERT as part of the mutual aid team." I point to the insignia on my shirt.

"Thank you for coming, obviously we need all the help we can get."

I don't like the way she says these words. It's almost as if she's thanking me for doing something big. This isn't big, it's what we signed up for. To help others.

"You don't need to thank me." I hold a tree limb back for her. "I knew what I was getting into when I joined. The last twenty-four hours have been something else though."

"Right?" She throws a grin at me. "I've never been equal parts scared and energized like that before in my life."

"I didn't know whether to take cover in the bathroom or run right out into it and immediately try to help," I agree. "There was something about listening to the ferociousness of it, but feeling the energy coming from it. I've never felt those before at the same time."

Even though it's dark, our eyes meet, illuminated by the flashlights both of us are carrying.

She licks her lips, her breathing slightly heavy. "Exactly."

We share a moment. Being the man I am, I'm not sure what kind it is. I've never been able to read women well, but there's a jolt of something between us. I can tell when she feels it, because she turns away from me.

"We should get going."

Her voice sounds almost disappointed.

I am disappointed. Even in the situation we're dealing with, I want to know more about what we just shared, but it's not the time.

For me it's never the time.

Five minutes we walk in complete silence, until we can hear people milling about and shouts of needing help. We look at one another, both picking up the pace. We're close when a large tree blocks our way.

"How are we going to get over it?" she pants, holding onto her side.

"However we can."

Gauging the distance, I move a little farther back, then take off at a run, pumping my arms and legs. I haven't run like this since my days on the football field. It feels amazing.

When I estimate I'm close enough, I push off with my feet, jumping high enough to grab hold on the top part of the log. I grunt as I pull myself up.

"Fuckin' pull-ups paid off." I shake my head, thinking of my dad and always telling us to do pull-ups.

Turning around, I see Rowan looking at me, her eyes wide, mouth open in the light she holds in her hands.

"Come on, you're wasting time. I'll lift you up, but you have to get a good running start."

This is it. The moment when I think she'll bow out and tell me she can't do this. It's what most women would do in her position, at least in my experience. But not Rowan, she puts her pack securely on her back, goes to where I started running, and takes off toward me. Her arms and legs are pumping so fast I almost don't see them.

"C'mon, c'mon," I encourage her. "Faster, just a little faster!"

Right when she gets to the part where I know she's got to let it fly, I scream. "Jump now!"

She does, lunging at me. I brace against the bark of the downed tree, gripping it tightly with the boots I'm wearing. My hand clasps hers tightly, heaving her up until I can get my arm around her waist. I grunt as I forcefully pull her up beside me.

"You good?"

She's sucking in great gulps of air, bent over at the waist; hands on her knees, but she nods. "I'm okay, just give me a minute."

"Take all the time you need. You did that like a boss. That was awesome!"

Her head lifts and she grins at me. "I wouldn't have done it if you hadn't done it first."

We're quiet again, both of us seemingly trying to prepare ourselves for what we're about to see. Trying to process what we've already seen.

"Okay, I'm ready."

Carefully I get us to the other side of the tree, before using a walkie talkie radio to let the others know there's another big tree in the way.

"Got it, Cutter." I hear Tucker's voice. "There are other workers coming up after y'all."

It's good to know we have backup, but first we have to get to the scene to know what we're going to have to do.

The closer we get, the louder it is. I wonder if this is what my dad dealt with when he was in the military. The screaming, the mass hysteria. I can feel it in my blood before I get there.

The fear, the unrest is almost a physical hum vibrating through my body.

Up ahead there's a clearing, and as Rowan and I walk through it, we're met with complete devastation.

"Shit," she whispers. "This was an apartment building."

It's leveled. Completely flattened to the ground.

The only thing recognizable is the wiring and metal that had once kept the building standing. It's in a heap like the Legos my nephew plays with. When he's done, he crashes what he's built, letting them lay in a pile of destruction in his aftermath.

Pushing thoughts of home out of my head, I try to assess the scene, try to figure out where we need to go first. Rowan is glancing around.

"Tonya!" she yells. "Where do you need us?"

The woman turns to the sound of Rowan's voice, her face screwing up in a sob. "Oh thank God you're here. We tried to get everybody to the basement, but then it started to flood." The woman is on this side of having a meltdown.

"You did all you could," Rowan soothes her. "Where do you need us? Who is hurt the worst that we can save?"

She whispers those words.

Tonya eyes her. "I don't want to make that decision."

Pulling a marker out of her bag, Rowan thrusts it to her. "You were an EMT for a lot of years. You have to make the decision. We can't save everybody, and you know it. Mark the ones we can, and start a triage."

"Ro, I can't," she whispers.

We're losing valuable and precious time.

"Look, none of us want to make decisions, but right now, it's a must. If we want to save even one person. We are obligated to do this. If you're an ex-EMT you're valuable and you can help your community. If you're not willing to do it, then get out of our way."

Her eyes cut up at me, but I let it roll off my back.

"If you aren't helping, you're a part of the problem."

Those words seem to push her into action.

"You've got this." Rowan squeezes her hand. "You've got this."

"I can't play God," she argues."

"You're not. You're making an informed decision. If he

and I try to do this, we'll end up losing more than we can save, because we'll want to save everyone. You've got to help us, otherwise this will never work."

The moment she decides, I can see it. Her chin tightens, her eyes become blank. It's the stare of someone who's separated themselves from reality so they can do what they must.

Whistling loudly, I get everyone's attention. "If you're injured, I want you to form a line behind Tonya." I point to the woman I haven't even had an introduction to yet. "She will be assessing you and sending you to either the left or the right. We're gonna do what we can to help, but you've gotta help us by remaining calm and patient. There are other first responders coming, but the way is blocked. It's going to take time. If you're not injured, please help where you're needed. If you have medical training, Rowan and I could use you. Let's get started."

I've seen a lot in my time, but one thing never fails to bring chills, and that's when people come together to help one another. Almost immediately what was chaos is getting organized. A few move forward telling me and Rowan they have some medical training, others form a straight line behind Tonya.

As she starts assessing, I bow my head down, whispering a prayer when I see her send the first one in line away from us.

There are so many who won't make it through the night, who didn't even make it through the storm. I vow right here and now to save who I can, and to provide comfort to those I can't. I won't get to everybody, but I'll do my best with the ones I come into contact with.

That's what I would want to happen to my family, and in times like these, we're all family.

CHAPTER FOUR

Rowan

FROM BENEATH MY LASHES, I watch him. This man from northern Alabama. He's different than I thought he would be. For some reason I assumed he would be the type of person to push me aside and insist he be the one to do everything. Instead he's given me my space to let me work. He's not crowded me, not asked me more than once if I need help, and he's been nothing but gentle to the people he's helped.

Cutter.

What an odd name, although I guess I can't say much, considering my own. Right now he's taking care of a small child, making the little girl laugh, even though she's going to need stitches in her foot. The wound is large enough I can see it from where I stand. It would have even an older person crying, but the tears she'd shed when he first picked her up and put her on a table we've procured, have stopped. They've turned into laughter because of him.

She looks like she's around four-years-old.

An iron fist squeezes my heart. The same way it always does when I see someone who reminds me of what I had for a brief time, and then lost.

"Am I good to go, Ro?"

My attention is brought back to the woman I'm working on. I've seen her around town, working at one of the shops on the strip. They're all gone now, or at least heavily damaged. Will she even have a job to go back to? My eyes close for a moment, trying to envision what her name tag said the last time I was there. Bridget. Her name is Bridget.

"You're good. Be sure to keep that clean and covered. If it starts to get red edges, any drainage, or you start running a fever, get to a doctor. It won't be hard to catch an infection in these conditions. Be safe, Bridget."

She grins, almost as if me knowing her name made her day. And maybe it has. I know better than most it's the little things that matter when the big things are fucked. And this? This is the most fucked this town has ever been.

"You too."

A glance at my watch shows we've been here for hours, waiting for others to relieve us. Even though I literally know how far they were behind us, I'm getting antsy. I need a way out of here that doesn't require me walking back the way we came.

We can hear our teammates now as they get closer. The roar of chainsaws and splitting wood provides an ear-splitting soundtrack to the mayhem we're trying to harness. I'm running out of supplies and we somehow need to get more. My back aches, sweat is trickling down my chest into the band of my bra. I want to reach down and wipe at it, but this is my last pair of gloves and they're covered in someone's blood.

"Open that." I point at a bottle of alcohol, as I instruct the next person in line. "Pour some over these gloves. It's the best we can do right now."

Even I know it's not good enough, but it'll have to do.

Glancing over at Cutter, our eyes meet. His mouth is set in as grim a line as mine. Trouble is going to come to us when we have to turn all these people away and there's no one here to help us.

He stands, stretching. The way his back pops makes me envy him. I can't do that without a chiropractor. My eyes roam his frame, looking at the tattoos, noticing the way the shirt clings to his muscular, yet lean body.

"Didn't you play at U of A?"

A man in the crowd walks up to Cutter, asking the question before he takes a seat. The body that had just relaxed into the back crack of the century is now stiff. It's obvious to everyone he doesn't want to talk about this. But the man must not take non-verbal cues well.

"A few games," he answers softly.

"Yeah, I remember. You lost your ride, right?"

"Not my proudest moment." Cutter shakes his head.

"I always wondered why, no one ever said and you were so talented. Never seen a kid run like you."

I feel bad for him. No one wants to hear all the things they could have done right, that they did so wrong. I know better than anyone.

"Made a mistake." He shrugs. "Lost my ride and had to come to terms with it. Decided to come home and be an EMT instead. Love what I do now."

He shoots me a look that says get me outta here but of course, I can't, so I just shoot him back a smile.

Cutter

THIS DUDE IS BUSTING my balls. Everybody thinks they know what the fuck I did to get kicked off the team, it's just not polite to talk about it in mixed company. At least I don't like to talk about it in any company.

Glancing over my shoulder I will the guys to work faster. The quicker I can get out of here and away from the watchful eyes of everyone, the better off I'll be.

"You're doing a great job." An older woman pats my shoulder.

"Thank you, ma'am."

She pinches my ass. Pinches. My. Ass.

I jump slightly, making a noise of surprise in my throat. Rowan, looks over at me, giggling.

Her laugh catches me off-guard. For as buttoned up as she looks, her laugh is loud and lyrical. I'd like to see what she looks like as she completely lets go of the obvious strong grip she has on herself.

Cutter, now's not the time.

That little voice in my head can shut the fuck up. When is the right time? Just as I'm about to ask for some water, judging by my line of thought, I need to hydrate, we hear the rest of the team finally getting through the tree over the road.

A loud cheer goes up when they're seen.

I may cheer myself. Back-up is finally here.

It's a lot of directing injured this way and that, filling our teammates in on what we've done while we've been separated, and unfortunately we have to call for the chaplain. Two people have died waiting for help to get here.

That's the hardest part, knowing we can't save everybody.

"C'mon, I think you and I have earned a rest."

She gets up, walking beside me. Again, I realize how much smaller she is than me, but as she stumbles, I rush to hold her up next to me.

"Sorry." She pushes her glasses, knocked askew, back up onto the bridge of her nose. "It's been a while since I ate."

I try to think back to the last time I did, but I can't seem to remember. This day feels like multiple ones all strung together.

"We'll find you something."

"No," she argues. "These people need it worse than I do."

Carefully, I turn her to face me, bending down at the knees so I can look her in the eyes. "Look, both of us are going to have to be on top of our game here, so we can help people. I'm hungry too, and I can't remember the last time I ate. If we don't take care of ourselves, we can't take care of anyone else."

She seems to listen to me, nodding slightly at what I'm saying.

"Cutter! You doing alright?" Tucker yells out.

I take the chance to wave him over. "We're okay, but both of us are pretty hungry. Any chance you can help with that?"

He nods to the truck we rode in. "There's a cooler in there with some snacks and some bottles of water. You two held it down for the rest of us to get here. Go take a break."

THE SILENCE in the truck is deafening. The quietness of it pops like gunshots in my ears. Rowan takes her glasses off, rubbing her eyes. She sighs heavily as she reaches around her neck, rubbing at the skin.

I can't take it any longer. I need to say something.

"Are you okay? Some of the stuff we saw back there was rough." For some reason I'm not as much worried about me as I am about her. She seems fragile, and I don't want the things we've seen tonight to cause her any bad feelings.

She looks up, almost as if she's forgotten I'm sitting here with her. She's startled, her hazel eyes huge as they close. "I've seen some stuff in my life. Things that have given me nightmares." She shakes her head. "I can honestly say I think this will be something I'll never forget."

I focus on chewing the peanut butter cracker I'm eating, trying to make sure I take the time to enjoy it. Back when I was cutting weight on the football field, this was something I would do to make sure I was able to savor my food.

When you're a college student on a scholarship and you require a lot of calories to cut weight and gain muscle, you learn every single trick there is.

"Yeah, I don't think I'll ever forget that lady's face when she had to tell the first person to go into the other line. Making the decision between life and death, playing God? We shouldn't have to be put in those positions. That'll stick with me for a while."

She takes a sip of her water, licking her lips to get the excess off. "It'll stick with her for a while too."

CHAPTER FIVE

Rowan

MY ALARM GOES off way earlier than I'm prepared for it to. For the duration of whatever this state of emergency is, we'll be working twelve-hours on and twelve-hours off, even with the help we're receiving from the LSERT.

As I turn over, my body protests. It isn't used to the level of physicality I pushed it to participate in last night.

Be honest, Ro, I chide myself. It's been a few years since you would have been sore for any other reason anyway. A person hasn't touched me other than to give me a hug since it happened and when I gave into my now-ex-husband one more time.

But that's neither here nor there right now.

Reaching out, I gasp; even my arm is sore. Probably from where Cutter lifted me up onto the tree. He's strong, and so damn sure of himself. I envy it and wish I was as sure of myself as he had been.

Cutter. That name again. That man. I close my eyes, seeing his face clearly.

I've never met someone like him. Never known someone to be as tattooed as he is, but also as soft-spoken either.

My phone makes a noise, letting me know I have a text. I'm not in the mood right now, but it could be something important.

"Ugh, Sullivan," I groan out as I see my brother's name on my phone.

S: How are you doing? I haven't heard from you since last night. Been worried.
R: Have you checked on Mom and Dad? I was a little busy.
S: Don't be a smartass, little sis. I was worried. And yes, I've checked on Mom and Dad, they're fine.
R: Then you should know just how tired I am right now.

I really don't wanna mess with him, and I'm slightly annoyed he's the first person I'm talking to this morning. I love him, don't get me wrong, but he's my brother and he can push every button I have.

If I had been a boy, I'd be working alongside my two brothers on the police force, but instead I'm an EMT. Dad subscribes to the old thought that policing is a man's job, and he never wanted me to be in harm's way. Funnily enough he didn't think about how he would protect me personally. Not to say I don't love my job, because I do. I honestly think I was born to do this, but there was definitely a favorite in my family, and it wasn't me.

S: I'm just making sure you're safe.
R: Well I am, you can run back and tell Mom and Dad I'm fine.
S: That's not why I'm messaging you, and you know it, you're just being ornery.
R: I love you, Sully. I'm just tired.
S: Love you too, Ro. See you tonight? I'm working.
R: I'm working overnight tonight, see you then.

Him mentioning work makes me wonder who's going to be working with us, which is surprising. I haven't been interested in anyone since I got divorced. Which is a story for another time. Immediately I wonder if Cutter's working.

"Rowan," I sigh as I speak to myself out loud. "Don't even think about it."

But I am, I'm thinking about possibly putting on a little makeup. We won't be responding to emergencies with the magnitude of what we did last night, but we'll still be responding if they need us.

Throwing my covers off, I push my legs over the side and put my feet on the floor. I'm one of the lucky ones who got to keep the roof over their head and also not lose electricity. For that I'm thankful, because I know how hot it is outside, and I'm cool here, inside.

When I get to the bathroom, I turn to the mirror, taking a look at myself. My waist is smaller than it ever has been, making my chest more obvious than it has been. I've been working out in my free time, and it's certainly paying off.

Which is a laugh. All my damn time is free.

Leaning forward, I suck in my cheeks, turning this way and that. Trying to see what someone else sees, but even I can't imagine. The person I'm looking at, I don't recognize and I'm not sure I ever did. She never looked at herself like this, and now I wonder why.

"DO you find me attractive as a man?" I abruptly ask Isaac later on that night. We're riding around, waiting to be called to a scene. There are still a lot of streets closed and certain parts of the town we won't even be able to get to, but we're still on standby ready to step in when called.

"As a man, no, you aren't attractive," he chuckles, shooting a look my way.

Jesus.

"Stop." I reach over, smacking him on the shoulder. "You know what I mean. If you were looking at me objectively - you know the way a man looks at a woman - am I attractive? Would you want to date me? Would you take a second look at me if we were walking down the street?"

He's squirming and I can tell I've made him uncomfortable, but there's two things. One, we went to high school together, and two, we've been partners for a while. I've had to listen a lot from him. Including him telling me about trying a threesome after a crazy night in New Orleans to where he is now with a wife and kid. The very least he can do for me is answer what I've asked.

"I mean, I think of you like my sister, Ro." He makes a face. "I'm probably not the best person to ask about this."

I get the feeling he's trying not to hurt mine. Which makes me even more suspicious and sends a sinking feeling deep in my stomach. It's doing nothing for my self-esteem, but I need to know. I need someone to talk to and right now he's the only one I got.

"If you didn't think of me like your sister," I huff, damn near begging. "C'mon, you know I haven't been on a date or even looked sideways at a man since I got divorced. I'm so far out of the loop, it's another country. Just give me an honest answer."

"Okay," he sighs, looking closely at me. I see him try to not be my friend, but be someone who might be interested in dating me. "You're cute."

That's exactly what I don't want to hear. Cute isn't what men like Cutter go for, I know that like I know the back of my hand. And here I go again, wondering what Cutter would like.

"I was a wife and a mother. When I think of cute, I think of someone with no past. Someone who's gone about life without any bumps in the road. I've had so many bumps that I they're nearly plastered on my forehead. If I were the undercarriage of a car, I'd be dragging the ground."

He stifles a laugh.

"Everybody has a past, Ro. Your past doesn't define you."

Easy for him to say. He doesn't have a hole in his heart that will never be filled, and he doesn't have to see his mistakes staring back in his face some days.

"I don't know."

"You do know," he insists. "You have every bit of confidence in your job. You know you can do it and there is no one who can make you feel inferior. When are you going to take that confidence to your personal life? It's been three years."

"To me it feels like three months, three days, maybe even three hours," I sigh. "I can't remember what she sounded like sometimes," I admit softly. "I have to pull up one of the videos I have on my cellphone. Her little laugh was the best." I grin.

"She got it from you."

"No, she didn't."

"Yes, she did. You haven't truly laughed in so long that you just don't remember what it sounds like."

I wonder, is he speaking the truth? Am I too close to the situation and I just don't see it?

"You've got to loosen the straps you use to hold yourself up to these high as hell standards you've adapted. Never having fun, never letting your hair down isn't the way the to memorialize her."

"I let my hair down."

His eyes cut at me. "Yeah, at night, before you go to bed. I haven't seen your hair down since high school."

This is the worst thing about living in a small town where everyone has known your whole life. "It tangles easily," I argue.

"Yeah," he laughs. "Just like life, Ro. None of it stays straight, life is meant to intertwine and weave. Our lives are one braid in a head of hair that makes up our whole story. Each of us is one strand, who do you want to be grouped with? It doesn't mean you're expected to spend your whole life being known as that curl too stubborn to straighten. It just means sometimes it takes a little prodding and that spray shit you girls like to use on your hair."

I shake my head. "Your analogy is insane, but believe it or not, I get what you're saying."

I've tried to make my life as separate from everything else as possible. No weaving, no getting so close to someone it would hurt when they left. When I lost my daughter and my marriage, I wasn't sure I'd ever recover. I'm not sure I can put myself out there again. Most people get a huge blow once in a lifetime, I got two at once.

Before I can think more about what a mess everything is, our radio is blaring. Meaning someone needs my help, and that's how I fill the loneliness now. By helping others and making sure I don't get too close.

CHAPTER SIX

Cutter

I'M DRAGGIN' ass. It's been the longest day we've put in since we got here. All I want is a cold beer and an even colder bed. My skin is burning like fire from the heat of the day.

But that won't be what I get.

Not to mean I'm not thankful. We at least have a roof over our heads and air conditioning. No matter how shoddy the AC is.

What I'm missing tonight are the cool sheets of my bed, slipping between them with nothing on, cranking up the AC in my bedroom, and turning my mind off to everything going on around the world.

I can't do any of those things right now.

Tucker and I are still rooming together, and I have to think he wouldn't be too happy with seeing anything I might inadvertently show while asleep. Our AC sucks, and the sheets are scratchy as fuck.

"You look done today."

"I am," I tell him as I enter the hotel room. Major comes over, giving me a sniff, before he licks my hand. It makes me smile, the first thing that's made me smile all day. "We pulled some bodies today," I say, my voice soft.

The bone-deep weariness finally gets the best of me, and I collapse onto my bed. It feels like I literally deflate.

It's taken everything I have in me to get through this day and I'm all out of fucks to give at this moment. When I signed up for the LSERT, my vision had obviously been short-sighted. I hadn't thought about disasters like this. About what it might do to me mentally, or even physically.

"Was that your first time?" he asks, his voice as soft as mine was when I told him.

"Yeah." I rub my hands through my hair. "Never had to do anything like that before."

"You'll never forget it." He rubs his head. "But you have to realize it has to be done."

Somehow the fact it has to be done makes me more pissed off. "It shouldn't need to be done."

Tucker looks at me, I can see the pity in his eyes. "The first time you realize how easy it is for life to be snuffed out, it's hard."

My head cocked to the side, I throw another question at him. "Are you insinuating eventually it won't be hard?"

"All I'm saying is at some point you realize this is the way life is. It's messy, it's painful, and it's unexpected. We fall in love when we don't mean to, we lose college contracts when it looks like our lives are perfect, and we witness the cycle of life and death, Cutter. It's just the way things are."

"Doesn't mean it's easy."

"It was never meant to be easy," he argues. "It's meant to

show us how to hang onto the good times, to make sure we understand how important it is to tell those we love, that we love them. It's meant to teach us life is finite. As much as we want to believe we're indestructible, we're not."

My throat is closing, tight from the unshed tears I can feel building behind my eyes. I clear it, before getting up and gathering my stuff to take a shower.

Time.

Time is what I need to process everything I saw today. There's a part of me that hates I have to take the time when others don't have the luxury.

My heart is pounding when I close the bathroom door behind me. My back hits it, and I do my best not to freak the fuck out. I've only had a panic attack once in my life before, and I feel another coming on now.

Quickly, I move over to the shower, cranking it on. It's a blur as I take my clothes off, then step under the spray.

It's freezing cold.

Almost as cold as my heart feels inside my chest.

Am I alive? Can I survive this?

The simple answer: I have to.

THE WATER DOESN'T EVEN FEEL cold anymore. It's lukewarm, maybe that means my body is still hot from the sun. Another part of me wonders if it's because the tears that've streamed down my face.

I've never been one to cry, even when my life hit the skids and I lost everything I thought was important to me.

But today, today broke me. Broke me in ways I'm unsure I'll ever be able to recover from. Slipping down to the floor of the bathtub, I pull my knees up to my body and close my eyes.

And I see it, just like I knew I would.

"Have you checked over there?" One of the EMTs from this area is pointing to a pile of bricks. Someone told me earlier this was an assisted living home for the elderly. Not a nursing home, but a place they could live out the rest of their lives as independently as possible. There are three people missing, and we haven't been able to find them yet.

There are only two more piles of bricks to go through.

As the day has gotten away from us, we've all become more tense, knowing there won't be someone we can administer first aid to. If we find someone, they will most likely have already perished.

"No." I shake my head, pulling the make-shift mask over my nose and mouth. "I'll go do it right now."

There's a feeling of foreboding. You know the one you get when you go into a haunted house attraction. Someone is gonna jump out and scare the absolute shit out of you, but you do it anyway, because you have to know how you'll react. That's kind of how I feel right now.

As I approach the rubble, I know what's about to happen. Every inch of my body knows it, my bones almost tingle with the knowledge.

I'm slow, because I don't want this to happen. In fact I want to be anywhere other than here. If I could trade places with anyone in the world right now, I would, no questions asked.

When I pry a large piece of brick, possibly part of the wall I see it. A lock of curly gray hair. The type of hair I imagine my mom will have when she gets to this age.

Time stops for me.

The sounds of everyone else working the scene goes away, and I go down to my knees, kneeling so that I can get a better look. A hand is reaching up over her head, frozen in time. A moment that will live on in my mind forever.

I take note of everything.

Her painted nails, the gorgeous engagement ring, a thoroughly loved wedding ring, and a watch that stopped at ten p.m. Not long after Hurricane Tatum made landfall.

My mouth is moving, but for some reason my throat won't work.

"I found someone." I can hear the words in my mind, but I know I didn't say them out loud. No one comes running to help me, in fact no one stops whatever they're doing. They're all going about business as usual.

"I found someone." I try again.

Still nothing.

There's a sick curiosity I have that needs to be satisfied. Is her husband with her? Did they at least die together? Why the fuck didn't they evacuate.

As I pull back more and more debris, I see exactly why.

He's in a wheelchair, and probably wasn't mobile. They probably couldn't evacuate. It looks like she was sitting on his lap, his arms wrapped tightly around her waist.

Bile rises up in my throat.

This could be my parents in a few years.

Quick as I can, I run from the rubble, before becoming violently ill.

This brings others to my side, all asking if I'm okay.

Not even a fucking little bit, but instead I answer.

"I'm fine, I found two of the three missing." I point over to where I had been, letting someone else do the rest of the job.

Now I wonder, did they have family?

Have they been notified?

Were they alone?

Did they have children who are worried?

Is no one waiting to hear if they made it through the storm?

All of the questions make my gut churn, and suddenly I'm way too hot to be in this room anymore. The water from the shower is pricking my skin and I can't fucking stand it.

When I step out, I see that the bathroom door is closed. Panic rises up my back and to my neck. I'm not even drying off before I put my clothes on and swing the door open. I inhale, huge gulps of air.

This air is recirculated from the room, but at least it doesn't have the musk of the bathroom. The humidity hanging so thickly in the air. Out here I don't feel like I'm about to pass the fuck out.

"Do we have any beer?" I ask quickly.

"Beer?" Tucker questions. "No, we don't have any beer. But I'd love some."

"I'll be back."

I don't even wait for him to say anything to me, I just take off, grabbing the keys to the truck and my wallet. For just a few moments I need the open road, a great song, and some fresh air.

For just a little while I need to pretend like today didn't happen and I'm the Cutter I was before I made this trip.

If I can't, I'm not sure I'll ever be able to find that Cutter again.

CHAPTER SEVEN

Rowan

THERE'S NOT MUCH open in town right now. Most of the stores and restaurants will take months, maybe even years to recover, if they even do. One place that always weathers the storm, is Shucker's, a family-owned barbecue joint.

It started as a little roadside spot, and in times of uncertainty, they revert back. It allows them to get food to people who need it, while still putting money into the community by paying others to work for them.

The parking lot is packed as I slow down, finding an empty space on the outskirts of the gravel. Grabbing my wallet and cellphone, I get out of the car, lock my doors, and go up to where the line is extended. Looks like many people had the same idea I did.

The group standing in line looks around as they wait. My high school English teacher sees me, and throws back a wave. "Hi Ro, thank you so much for helping at the apartment building. One of my fellow teachers was there and said how much they appreciated you."

I grin, happy to hear we were able to make a difference. "It's my pleasure." I lift my hand in a wave back to her.

The person in front of me turns around. The first thing I get a look at is a ton of tattoos, and even if we hadn't been in a life or death situation, I still would have taken the time to see what kind of tattoos they were.

"Cutter." I nod, glancing up into those green eyes.

"Rowan, how are you?"

The tone he uses as he asks the question makes me wonder if he really wants me to answer it. Something pricks at the back of my neck. Like maybe he's only asking because manners force him to. The way his gaze doesn't stay locked on mine is a clue he's not really interested.

So I give him an answer that's not completely the truth.

"I'm good."

When in reality I'm so far from good, I might as well be on the other side of the planet. "What are you doing here?"

His eyebrow quirks in surprise. Obviously he didn't expect me to be on the asking questions end of this conversation tonight.

"Hungry." He shrugs. "Needed a beer." His head tilts to the menu which has drink options on it. Then I watch a physical change in him, almost like he couldn't hold up the pretense any longer. His shoulders slump, and this time when he speaks, his tone is truthful with a touch of vulnerability. "Had to get out of that fucking hotel room. It was starting to close in on me."

I know the feeling all too well.

Even though he and I just met literal days ago, I still

need to ask him, to make sure he's okay. "Do you want to talk about it?"

For a few seconds those eyes of his cloud, like he's remembering something so painful it physically hurts. Then the look is gone and he shakes his head. "No, not right now, anyway."

I can relate and respect what he's saying. I haven't mentioned her name since she died. Haven't been able to, and I'm not sure when it'll change. I stopped counting the days because the numbers were getting so big. With the devastation of the hurricane, I just can't keep doing it to myself.

Failure was starting to swirl in my stomach, and I couldn't take it any longer. I'd already failed so much. More of the same was too big of a burden to bear.

The line is moving swiftly, and soon we're the next two in line.

"Would you like to eat with me?" Cutter asks. "I don't want to go back to that hotel room, but I don't want to eat a meal alone either. I go back and Tucker'll be talking to his wife. I'll have worried text messages from my mother and sister-in-law. Tonight I just can't handle it. Please say you'll eat with me."

Because I understand more than I can ever express, I nod my head yes.

Before I realize it, I've ordered along with him, and he's paying for my meal.

"You didn't have to do that." I reach into my wallet, pulling out enough to cover my share; wings and a bottle of Coke.

"No." He pushes my hand away. "You're doing me a

favor by agreeing to eat with me. There's no way I'm gonna take your money, Rowan."

"Well at least let me pay you back somehow."

I don't feel comfortable letting him pay without knowing I can return the favor.

"Tomorrow night? Dinner again? It's nice to have company other than Tucker and Major. He's the epitome of family togetherness while I'm the epitome of single and not-yet ready to mingle."

I laugh, throwing back my head, because I never expected to hear those words out of his mouth. "Sure, why not?"

For a few minutes we stand in silence while we wait for our food. I'm interested in why he's not-yet ready to mingle. From the outside looking in, he seems to have it all together, doesn't appear to have any of the hang-ups most men his age do.

But that's the problem with looking in. A lot can be hidden when you're just looking in. Once you get past the curtain, really see in the window, and get to know a person, there's more than you ever could have imagined. I mean look at me and what I'm hiding. It's enough for an entire episode of Dr. Drew.

Our number is called, and while Cutter goes to get our food, I'm tasked with finding us a place to sit.

Since most establishments are still closed, Shucker's has added a bunch of picnic tables to the few they already had. If I had to guess there's at least twenty set up out here. Most are full, but I see one at the very back. A small family has just gotten up from it, so I head over in that direction, putting my wallet on the table as I have a seat, throwing my leg over the bench.

Lights are starting to pop on around this eating area. Glancing at the screen on my phone, I see it's going on eight o'clock. Looking at the sky stars starting to appear, and the sun is setting in the distance. A bright pink hue bleeds into the blue/gray of the night canvas. This would be a perfect picture, but I've stopped taking them.

They don't help when your dream is ripped from you and all you have left are memories. You look at those pictures and wonder why you didn't live in the moment. Why you were so worried about getting a picture when the memory could have lasted just as long.

"Here we go."

Shaking my head slightly to clear those thoughts, I try to get back to where I was before I came over here to sit. Cutter doesn't know my history, doesn't know that I sometimes get lost in my own head, and right now it'd be weird to explain it to him. If anything, I'd rather have a friend who didn't know. At least then I'd know they didn't hang around me out of pity.

"This looks so good." I give him a smile, genuinely happy to be having a meal with someone other than my family or my partner.

"Do they normally have a bigger set up?" Cutter asks as he digs into a sandwich.

I notice he's also got some wings. I love a man who can chow down on wings.

"Yeah." I dip my meat in the ranch dressing I ordered and take a bite. "They actually have one of the lots in downtown."

He whistles, knowing a lot of downtown was completely destroyed.

"Exactly." I take a drink of my Coke. "They started out

here though, and they typically keep it open in the summer to help serve the beach crowds. Every hurricane that's come through here or tornado we've had, they've always opened this place up. There's one thing you can count on in the face of tragedy, and it's that Shucker's will be open. If it wasn't, I don't know what we'd do."

"It's amazing this little building withstood the force of the storm." Cutter looks out at the parking lot, seeing the beach from where we sit.

"Because of the natural barriers." I point out the fact it's on a hill, there's a windbreak of trees, and the little shack is nestled into almost an alcove. "This place has withstood the test of time; it may not look like much, but this right here? It's the heart of this community. Without it, I don't know what we'd be doing."

"Eating sandwiches and chips in the hotel room," he jokes.

But me, I'm thinking of another time. When I had nowhere else to go, I came here that night. They fed me, they told me everything was going to be okay, and that had been the first time I believed it. The first time I could see a way out of what had happened.

"This is definitely better than that. Tomorrow, I'll have to get some of the mac and cheese for you to try. It's won awards."

He groans. "I'm looking forward to it."

So am I, but I can't say that words. I don't want to give myself false hope that maybe, just maybe, the exile I've been in is potentially coming to an end.

Instead, I give him another grin and get to work on my plate of food. Eating means not talking, and right now that sounds good to me.

CHAPTER EIGHT

Rowan

"JUST LET ME HELP YOU." Isaac tells the man we're attending to. He's been fighting our intentions since we showed up.

"Please," I beg. "Let us look at the wound."

The call came in as a man who had been cleaning up from the hurricane. Sheet metal is still wrapped in trees, and some came falling down on his head. There's a very deep abrasion, and it's bleeding profusely. Not horribly alarming with head wounds, but we've got to make sure there's no underlying conditions.

"I don't need no goddamn help. I'm fine."

Isaac looks up at me, his cheeks going red. He's about to lose it. That's the sign. "You're not fine," he argues.

A patrol car pulls into the driveway behind our ambulance. A sigh of relief escapes my chest. We need help with this man. He's not listening to us, so hopefully he'll listen to whoever's come to our rescue.

"Y'all havin' issues?"

Of course it's my brother. I turn around, hand on hip, eyes ready to roll when I see someone else has stepped out of the patrol car with him. He's not riding alone. At first I think my eyes are playing tricks on me. He's an EMT, not a cop. But as they get closer, I see everything.

The dark hair.

The tattoos.

The soulful eyes that teeter on the edge of dark and light.

Kinda how I think he teeters on the edge sometimes between good and bad.

Between what's right and what feels good.

Last night I had a great time with him, and I'm looking forward to tonight. I thought about him way more than I should have when I got home.

As he approaches, putting one foot in the front of the other, the authoritative swagger I would recognize anywhere as his - after all it was ingrained when he pulled me over that tree trunk - cause me to pull my bottom lip between my teeth. Something about the way his hips roll. Equal parts relaxed and ready to move if he needs to.

Just like that, a part of me that hasn't been alive in three years takes notice.

And if I'm not mistaken, Cutter has taken notice, too.

They come to the rescue, helping Isaac get this man under control. When he's finally sitting on the stretcher in the back of the ambulance, he takes a look at all of us.

"Don't want y'all to help me," he sneers. "Would rather have the pretty lady within grabbing distance."

He makes a vulgar gesture with his hand. One that irritates me, but I'm used to them. My brother though? He's not used to seeing it at all.

"Hey, don't disrespect her like that." He presses back on the man's shoulder. "You show her some respect."

Isaac stands to the side, his arms folded over his chest. He's obviously had enough of this himself. Honestly, right now, the last thing I want to do is help this man. I'm torn between my duty and annoyance.

"I'll do this." Cutter grabs a pair of gloves.

"Said I want her," the man argues.

"Nope." Cutter shakes his head. "You lost your chance with her. Now you get me. So lean back and let me look at you."

The tone of his voice leaves no room for disobedience. Something I feel acutely between my thighs.

So not appropriate.

I try not to let them, but my eyes roam Cutter's back, watching as he examines the patient. The shirt he wears is one that's seen a lot of washes, given the way it molds completely to the muscles and contours.

What the fuck is happening with me? One dinner with the man and I've turned into the main character of a romance movie.

"He's gonna have to go to the hospital." Cutter grimaces. "It's a pretty deep cut."

Looking down, I see the blood splatter on his gloves.

"I don't want to go!"

"Too bad," my brother cuts him off. "You're going because I say you're going."

"I'll ride back here with him," Cutter offers.

"Good enough for me." Isaac had enough before we even got here. He throws his gloves off and heads for the driver's seat.

"Go ahead." Cutter nods to me with his head. "Wait up there."

I don't want to. It's my job to stay back here with our transports. I'm normally the one who does this, and I don't feel right letting someone else do it, even if I know they should. Sullivan catches my arm, our eyes meeting.

"Do as he says. I don't trust this guy."

If anything Sullivan has always had my best interest at heart. Even when we were little kids who argued over every single thing. If there's anyone I trust, it's him. Glancing back at the three of them, I leave the back of the ambulance, going to my seat in the passenger side.

"You okay?" Isaac asks as I get situated.

I'm watching the sideview mirror for Sullivan to come out. When he does, I breathe a sigh of relief. "I'm fine."

"He was way out of line with the gestures he was making and the way he was talking."

"You act like it's the first time I've ever seen or heard someone do those times of things. You know better than anyone how often I've dealt with it."

"Still doesn't mean I have to like it."

Sullivan taps the side of our ambulance, indicating it's time for us to go.

"THANKS FOR YOUR HELP." Isaac slaps Cutter on the back after we get the man wheeled into the ER. "I know I shouldn't let it, but people like that sometimes get to me."

"It's one of the worst parts of the job," Cutter agrees. "I didn't mind to help, that's what I'm here for."

All three of us walk outside. The sun is starting to lower,

causing me to take a look at my watch. "We're off," I tell my partner. "If you wanna drive the ambulance back, I think I'd rather walk."

It's a little over a mile to the ambulance bay and sometimes I enjoy the way a walk after a hectic day can calm me down.

"Mind if I join you?" Cutter questions. "I could definitely use the exercise."

Part of me doesn't believe what he's saying because he's in such good shape, but who am I to deny a walk?"

"Sure."

Isaac and I have a conversation between gazes. We don't say a word, but with my eyes, I let him know I'm okay with Cutter.

"I'll see you in a couple of days." He salutes, jogging back to the ambulance.

"Couple of days?"

We take off walking. "Isaac and I don't work again for three days. This is our weekend. Now that some of the cleanup has started and most of the emergent issues have been taken care of, they're putting us back on regular schedules. Especially since a lot of us had so much overtime the first couple of nights. When I clock out I'll have worked eighty-five hours this week. That includes the all-nighter we pulled."

"I didn't realize you'd done that much." He puts his hands in his pockets, measuring his gait to mine.

I'm sure he wants to walk faster, but my legs are much shorter than his. The day is muggy and warm, but full of the promise of a coming fall. Sweat makes my glasses slip slightly down my nose. I reach up, pushing them back to where they need to be.

"I didn't even think about it, truth be told." I shrug. "It had to be done, people needed help and that's what I'm here for."

"But still, it's gotta be exhausting."

A chuckle pushes out of my mouth. "You tell me, you've been working the same kinda shifts we have."

"Not really." He shakes his head. "I go home to a motel room where I ain't expected to clean a damn thing. You must have someone else to clean up after."

My smile is wistful. "Not anymore. Just me, and even though my apartment is lived in, I enjoy keeping things in their places."

"Ms. Type A. I can see that."

"Type A?" I huff. "Whatever, I'm not Type A. I don't always have to have everything right where it's supposed to be."

"Oh yeah." He turns to face me. "In the few days I've been here, I've not seen your hair down once."

Because my hair up is my security blanket.

"It's long, heavy, and gets tangled," I protest. "It's easier to keep it up when I'm working."

He raises a brow. "But I've seen you when you've not been working."

I struggle to find another answer. "It's hot."

"Alright Rowan, but one day," – he reaches over to tuck an errant strand behind my ear – "I'm gonna need the real answer as to why you don't wear your hair down."

A non-comital hum is all I give him. We turn into the parking lot of the ambulance garage. "I'm gonna need a ride back to the hotel, if that's cool."

"Yeah, no problem."

"We can stop and get that mac and cheese you promised me," he reminds me. "There's a lobby with tables."

It's against my better judgement, mostly because I haven't had to use it in the past four years, but the next words coming out of my mouth are unexpected, even from me. "I have a balcony on my apartment, and I'm lucky enough to have air conditioning right now. We can eat there."

His eyes roam mine, looking for I'm not sure what.

"Do you mind if I shower? The shower in the hotel is awful, and I've been out in this all day."

There are sweat stains on his shirt I must have previously overlooked, his skin tinted red from the sun.

"Don't mind at all."

But in my head, I'm saying, *Stupid, stupid girl.*

CHAPTER NINE

Cutter

"I'LL BE RIGHT BACK, just have to run up and get my stuff."

I hope Rowan doesn't bolt. She kinda looks like she wants to take away the invitation she gave to shower at her apartment. Can't say as I'd blame her, but I really hope she doesn't.

"Take your time."

That's the last thing I'm going to do. Rushing into the lobby, I see a ton of people waiting for the elevator. Fuck that. I ran enough stairs during football, I can beat the elevator. A quick look around shows me where the stairwell is, and up I go, taking them two at a time. All because I don't want her to leave.

Getting to our room, I fumble with the key card. When I finally get it open, I burst through it, almost running over Major.

"Why in such a big hurry?" Tucker mumbles from where he lies face down on his bed. He worked a long shift yesterday and I'm not surprised he isn't awake yet.

"Having dinner with Rowan and she's letting me take a real shower at her house."

"I hate you." He flips me the bird without opening his eyes. "The water pressure on that fucking thing is from World War II."

"I know, love you." I blow kisses at him. "Don't wait up."

Luckily for me I haven't taken much out of the bags I came here with, so it's easy to transfer everything into a small one. I head to the door with a loud "screw you" yelled my way.

It's fine, I'll take the abuse any day to hang out with the girl. I'm out, and heading down the stairs as quickly as I can. When I broach the entrance, I'm fully aware there's a possibility she may have left. Maybe I came on too strong, asking her to borrow her shower. Too late for me to take it back now, though.

My eyes adjust to the sun still shining and my heart thunders. I don't see her anymore. She must have left.

I'm dejected, turning back to go the way I came.

"Cutter!"

It's her voice. The urgency in it causes me to turn back around.

"Where are you going?"

I grin, walking over to where she's driving up. "Thought you left me."

"No," she laughs, shaking her head. "I had to make a circle because I was in the way of some other people. I got honked at." She rolls her eyes.

"Then you turned around and honked at me."

"You looked so dejected." She stops at the sign engaging her turn signal before trying to merge onto the main road. "Like I'd hurt your dog or something, your shoulders were slumped."

"I'm looking forward to spending time with you," I admit.

She glances over at me, the air conditioning blowing her hair. The voice she speaks with is lower than I'm used to. "I'm looking forward to it, too."

"IT'S NOTHING SUPER FANCY," Rowan says as we go up the stairs to what I assume is her apartment.

"Anything's better than the hotel. It's so impersonal. I miss my own bed," I admit.

Being away from home has been harder than I thought it would be. Even though I'd done it in college. It's been years now since I've been away. I'm used to going and seeing my mom and dad whenever I want to, dropping over at Ransom's to see my nephew. Throwing balls with Rambo. Dinner at The Café. I miss it more than I thought I would.

"If I were you I'd be missing my own bed too. I don't know how you're doing it, I'm not sure I could be away from my family."

"It helps having Tucker here. He and I have known each other for a long time. In a few weeks we'll be relieved or joined by other members of the LSERT."

"Any of your family?" She stops in front of a door with a wreath on it, which proclaims her a fan of Auburn.

"Damn girl." I push my fingers through my hair. "You were the perfect woman, but you're not a fan of Alabama? My heart is broken."

Her eyes squint with anger. "You're a fan?"

"I fucking played football for them."

She stands with her hands on her hips. "Does this mean we have to discontinue our friendship?"

That's the last thing I want to do. "I'll be okay with it as long as you're okay with it."

"I guess I won't hold it against you if you don't hold it against me." She holds out her hand.

I look down, grabbing it with my own.

There's a shock between the two of us. One I've never felt before, that I've always heard I would. All the guys I work with have told me about it and I'd know when I did. Back as a youngster in college, I thought I'd felt it, but what I just shared with Rowan? It's so much stronger than what I did back then.

We're staring at each other, and as my brown eyes meet her blue, I can see she felt it too. Neither one of us will be ignoring this, there's no way we can. Doesn't mean we're gonna act on it right this second, but we're going to.

There's no way in hell we can't.

We enter her apartment, and I'm hit with the smell of apple cinnamon.

"Smells like freaking apple pie in here." I rub my stomach.

"My mom dropped one off last night," she points to her fridge. "I'll warm us up a piece with dinner. She sent some vanilla ice cream with it, too."

"Holy shit, I have such a huge sweet tooth. I think I may have just fallen in love with your mother."

She laughs loudly, her head throwing back with the force of the noise. "She's easy to fall in love with. I'm pretty sure over half the county's in love with her already."

Reaching behind me, I scratch my neck. "That shower?"

"Oh yeah, sorry."

"I don't want to seem ungrateful, but I stink."

"We both do. I'll take one after you."

Immediately my mind goes to places it shouldn't. Imagining her naked, against the wall, water rushing over her bare body. I've never had such a visceral reaction to another woman. Surprisingly it doesn't even scare me. Maybe, just maybe I'm finally ready for this portion of my life.

"THERE'S TOWELS IN THE CLOSET." She points to a little alcove past the door. "You're welcome to use anything you need, but something tells me you don't want to use my strawberry bodywash."

With a chuckle, I wink. "I'm secure enough in my manhood to smell like fruit."

"Thank God for that."

The little flash of personality is one of the best things I've ever heard. She shuts the door behind her, leaving me on my own for the first time in a while. Acutely, I realize how long it's been since I've been alone. Really alone, with nothing else to do. Not since before I came here. Even at home people needed things from me. All Rowan wants is my company, and I'm more than happy to give her this piece of myself.

Reaching into the shower, I turn the knob, letting the water come on. The water pressure is already more than I hoped for. Stepping under the spray, I moan loudly, letting the warmth flow over my sore muscles. Sore from the work we've been doing and the bed I've been sleeping on. I really want my pillow top, king-size mattress back along with the mountain of pillows I use. The two flat ones I get at the damn hotel aren't even enough to keep my head off the bed.

As much as I want to stay in here for hours, I'm aware Rowan needs to get in here too, and let's face it, I want some of that pie and ice cream. Getting out, I dry off quickly, putting on a pair of athletic shorts and leaving my shirt off. It's been an amazingly hot day, and all I want is to let my skin breathe.

Opening the door, I'm pushing the towel through my hair as I step into the hallway. "Your turn."

As I walk ahead, I bump into something, immediately knowing it's Rowan. My hands find her hips so that I can keep her from falling. Her hands grip my biceps.

"I'm so sorry." I drop the towel. "I'm used to living alone, and there's hardly ever anyone around when I take a shower. I come out drying off my hair all the time, it's a bad habit. I should have thought more about where I am."

"No." She reaches up, forking her fingers through my hair, pushing it back on the top. "It's okay."

"It's long." I glance up at my bangs. "Wish I'd had a chance to get it cut before I came down here. It makes it that much hotter."

"I can cut it for you," she offers.

"What do you not do?"

"Gardening." She winks. "I suck at gardening."

"That's good." I dip my head down to hers. "Good to know. At least now I know I can bring you flowers. Something you can't get for yourself."

Her cheeks turn a bright pink and I want more than anything to take those glasses off, and kiss her silly, but now's not the time. It's coming, but it's not here just yet.

I'm a patient man, and I don't care if I have to wait.

CHAPTER TEN

Rowan

"SO" – I push back from him with my hands on his shoulders – "I called in our food, and they're gonna deliver it. They treat first responders really well. If you could listen for it while I go take a shower?"

"No problem." He lets go, but hangs on until the last moment his fingertips can. "Promise I won't be too nosey."

There's a lurch in my chest, but I know instinctively I can trust him. "I only have like one major secret." I shrug. It gives off the vibe I'm kidding, I know that, and Cutter takes it the way I mean for him to.

"I'll try not to let you break my heart," he laughs.

There's something prophetic about his words that hit me in the sternum. Almost as if it's a place we're going and I need to protect him from my past. "You do that."

He pulls back slightly, his eyes drawing together.

"I'll be back in a few."

As quickly as I can, I make my getaway, thankfully closing the door to the bathroom and pressing my back against it. In the last three years I haven't worried about how my previous life experiences would affect someone else. The truth is I haven't had to, I've not let anyone get close. But Cutter? Cutter is someone I want to get to know, someone I want to let get close. He's the kind of guy I can imagine a life with. Funny when he wants to be, serious when he needs to be, willing to help instead of watching from the sidelines like *he* did. *He didn't even try to help me save her*.

I grit my teeth as I let those thoughts loose, enjoying the pain for a moment. It reminds me that I'm alive. Tears spring to my eyes, and I angrily shove them away. There's no reason to get overly emotional. Not right now, not with this guy outside in my living room.

But I close my eyes. Think of her dark curls, her blue eyes, and the way she smiled up at me like I was everything to her. I want someone to smile at me like that again. I want to be an important part of someone's life one more time. Give me a damn reason to wake up in the morning.

Letting out a breath, I walk over to the shower, turn it on, and let the rush of the water drown out the rush of tears falling from my eyes.

"THAT NECKLACE." I point to the one around Cutter's neck. We're eating the food that was delivered while I was in the shower. "What is it?"

He looks down, hooking it around his thumb. "My older brother, Ransom, gave it to me when I tested for my certification and got my license to be an EMT, then a paramedic. It's Saint Michael the Archangel, I always wear it. He's the patron saint for police officers, paramedics, and the military. Weirdly enough in any situation I'm in, whether it's dangerous or not, I feel safe."

"So is that why you were able to make a run toward the apartment building without even thinking twice about it?"

"Yeah." His mouth quirks up in a grin. "I don't even think twice about it."

"I wear one too," I lift up the necklace holding a small vial of Etta's ashes. I don't tell him what it is. "It helps me to save the ones I can, and hopefully let go of the ones that I can't."

He nods, not asking, which I'm grateful for, but the silence is too awkward for me.

"How much older is your brother than you?"

I want to know everything I can about the man sitting across from me, making quick work of the BBQ in front of him.

"Three or four years, depending on what part of the year we're in."

"What does he do?"

I reach down to take a bit of my BBQ, putting it atop some of the cornbread.

"He's a K-9 Handler for Laurel Springs PD. He and Rambo are pretty well-known throughout the state."

"Oh my God!" I work hard to chew the food in my mouth, then swallow quickly. "I've heard of Rambo."

"Yeah." Cutter grins, a high-pitched voice I never thought I'd hear from him coming out. "He's a very good boy."

I giggle, before reaching over to take a drink of my sweet tea. "Do you talk to him like that all the time?"

"It's mandatory." He takes a drink of the bottle of beer I ordered him. "He doesn't respond unless you do. He wants all the praises he can get."

"Just like a man." I smirk. "Is he your only sibling."

"Yeah, my dad was older when my parents had kids, so they stopped at us. We were fuckin' hellions, though. There's no way they could have dealt with more."

"Why am I not surprised?"

"We do calm down though. My brother's proof of it. He's married now with a kid and a house, and they've got the dog. They're living the American dream."

"A kid?" My ears perk up.

"Yeah." Cutter reaches over, grabbing his phone off the table. "Keegan's my nephew." He pulls up a picture of the two of them. They're in a pool and Cutter has the toddler on his shoulders. They're both laughing and smiling like they have no cares in the world.

"The two of you seem like you have a lot of fun."

"Yeah." His tone is wistful. "I miss him. He's my buddy. We do a lot together. Ransom and his wife, Stella, are both on the frontlines so to speak. She's an RN, so their shifts are crazy. I watch him as much as I can so they can have time together. Ransom is so pussy-whipped it's not even funny."

I do everything I can not to spit out the bite of mac and cheese I just took, choking as I manage to get it down.

"Too crass?" His eyes are sparkling.

"No." I take a long drink, trying to catch my breath. "Just can't say I expected it in those terms."

"He loves her, don't get me wrong. They love each other

like one of those fucking Nicholas Sparks books that everyone reads, but he's totally whipped."

I give him a grin. "So you wouldn't be."

"I mean," – he makes a face – "depends on how good it is with the woman I choose."

"You're something else." I clear my throat, going back to my food.

"You've asked me all the questions," he says. "By the way, you were right about this mac and cheese, it's the best thing I've eaten in a while."

"Told ya!"

"How about your family?"

This is where it gets dicey for me, where I wonder what I should reveal and if anyone even really cares. So I keep it simple, just like I always do. "My parents have been married for almost thirty years. He's the Chief of Police. I have two brothers. You've met Sullivan, and the other one, Braylon, is at the PD too, but he sustained an injury and is riding the desk until his knee heals from surgery. I'm the youngest."

"I bet they protected you like crazy."

They tried.

"Yeah, it was hard to bring home someone I wanted to date, they'd be assholes about it every single time."

"Sullivan seems like a cool dude though, the little I've come to know him. He thinks a lot of you."

A snort escapes my nose. "Did he warn you off and all that jazz?"

"Nope, he told me you'd overcome a lot and he's proud of where you are."

My heart pounds and my hands start to shake. "What did he tell you about what I've overcome."

His dark eyes see everything. I can tell they do. They

look through me like there's nothing between us. Not even the clothes I wear.

"Nothing, and I didn't ask. It's not my place. If you ever want to tell me the things you've had to deal with, that's your business, Ro."

The nickname everyone has used since I was a kid sounds sexier sliding off his lips, in the deep tone of his voice. Appetite gone, I notice he's eaten everything in front of him. "Since we're done with dinner, do you want me to cut your hair, then we can have dessert?"

At the mention of dessert, the mood in the room shifts, for both of us. The air gets heavy, and we're both aware of the implications of what dessert can mean.

"I mean the apple pie." I smirk.

"I know what you meant." He smirks back. "I would really appreciate it if you'd cut my hair."

I stand up, stretching my back, moaning slightly when it pops. "Let's go out to the balcony. That way if we make a mess it won't take long to clean it up. I'll be there in a second, let me go get my shears."

He nods, taking his bottle of beer with him.

I walk slowly back to the bathroom, rummaging through my stuff for the shears I use to cut Sullivan's hair, along with the comb. My hands are shaking, and my stomach is full of butterflies.

Glancing at myself in the mirror, I almost don't recognize who I've become. The regular Rowan never has this touch of color to her cheeks, this brightness in her eyes. I almost put my hair down, but it's the security blanket I've always had. I can't let him in that far, not just yet.

Blowing out a breath, I pad back toward the balcony, the shorts I wear rubbing irritably on my thighs. Even that is enough to turn me on right now. As I approach Cutter from behind, I can see him reach down, adjusting his crotch slightly and I can't help it. A triumphant smile covers my face. A confidence I haven't had in years flows through my veins.

"You ready?" I announce my presence. "This should only take a few minutes."

His gaze is lazy as it washes over me from head to toe. "Take your time, I'm not in a rush."

And neither am I. Neither am I.

Cutter

HER FINGERS RUNNING through my hair is the best thing I've felt in years. I can't help but moan as she combs through it, moving my neck along with the motions of her stroking.

"Feel good?" she whispers.

I swallow roughly. "Yeah, you have no idea."

Judging by the way she keeps her mouth closed, but continues to run herself all over me, she does have some sort of idea.

"How's this?"

My eyes pop open, I can't believe she's done. It feels like she just started, but when I look down I see large clumps of hair. She's obviously been working for a while. A mirror is in front of my face. Honestly, no matter what she's done here, I'll appreciate it, but I make a deal out of looking this way and that. "Looks good, thank you so much."

"No problem." She grins.

It's the type I haven't seen on her face yet. One part flirty, part proud of herself. "How about that dessert?"

Her grin tilts lopsided. "Oh, I guess we can eat dessert."

As I watch her walk back into the kitchen, I wonder what's going on inside that head of hers, because all I know is mine is racing a hundred miles a minute.

CHAPTER ELEVEN

Cutter

"I'M gonna send you back out with Sullivan today." The man in charge of our assignments points at me. "He's gonna be checking some of the outer edges of town. You should be there in case there needs to be medical attention rendered."

"Got it." I go to the locker they've given me to work out of. Reaching in, I have my go bag. It's second nature to check it, making sure I have everything I need to render aid. This has been mostly what I've done since the night I helped Rowan. Different than what I thought, but no less important. I love helping the people of this state, and Paradise Lost reminds me a lot of Laurel Springs.

Right as I have that thought, a request for a FaceTime comes through from Stella.

"Hello?" I answer, smiling immediately when I see Keegan. "Oh my God, Bub, you're so much bigger than you were a week and a half ago!"

"Isn't it crazy?" Stella laughs as she tries to avoid his

hands, grabbing for her phone. "He's hit a growth spurt. Say hi to Uncle Cutter." She points to my face in the phone.

"Hi!"

"I miss you so much, Bub."

"We miss you too." Stella gives me a look in the phone. "Your parents are worried, and so is Ransom. Neither one of them will say anything. You know how they are. I'm just checking to make sure you're doing okay."

"I'm good, Stelle, I promise. It's different," I admit. "But we're doing good work."

"You look good." She scrutinizes my hair. "You get your hair cut?"

Leave it to her.

"I can't believe they have barber shops open down there."

"People gotta make a living."

She tilts her head. "Why do I get the feeling you're lying to me?"

"Don't know, maybe you're just distrusting."

"And maybe you're an a-hole."

I chuckle. "I see you're still not able to cuss around big ears." I point down to Keegan.

"Don't even get me started. We had dinner with my parents last night, and let's just say Ransom let him watch something he shouldn't have. I've never been so embarrassed in front of my parents, and that's saying something."

I can only imagine.

"Cutter, you ready?"

Looking back at Sullivan, I nod. "Be right there."

"Gotta go. Love you, Bub!"

"Love you!" he parrots back, waving his left hand enthusiastically. He's gonna be a south paw. Ransom and I are excited.

"Love you, Cutter. Stay safe!"

"You too, tell everybody I love 'em and I said hi."

Quickly I disconnect the call and get ready to go with Sullivan. Hefting my bag over my shoulder I meet him out in the lobby. "Ready when you are."

Today he brings me to a SUV, instead of the patrol car we went to before.

"We're going into more secluded area, we can't be sure it's been cleaned up. This is the last place we go when natural disasters hit," he says by way of explanation.

I'm aware of these places, far away from the main vestiges of civilization. We have them in Laurel Springs. They're the people who don't necessarily want the help from police and first responders alike, but we still offer it. It's part of the oath we take.

"Might be a rough ride, just be prepared," he warns.

Nodding, I get in the SUV, securing myself in the passenger side.

We've been driving for fifteen minutes when Sullivan speaks. "Was that your wife and kid on the phone?"

"Wife and kid?" I question, then I remember talking with Stella and Keegan. It causes me to crack up. "Oh hell no!"

"I didn't think it was that funny of a question to ask." His irritation is palpable. "I've heard you're hanging out with my sister. Can't blame a brother for checking. She's been through enough shit."

I definitely want to ask about the shit she's been through, but I'd rather ask her about it. Instead, I put his fears to rest. "That was my sister-in-law and nephew. She's married to my older brother, but she treats me like she's my mother half the time."

Realization shines in his eyes. "Makes sense. I'm glad to know you aren't fuckin' my sister over."

"There's no fuckin' going on, over or otherwise," I snap, without really meaning to. "But if there were, that's our business and not yours."

A small smile spreads across his lips. "You're gonna do just fine with her, Cutter."

God, I hope so.

"FEEL like we're gonna be running into a swamp soon," I joke with Sullivan as we go over a road we can't see. It's still covered with water, but he's assured me we'll make it.

"Watch for gators, never know what the hurricane washed up. That's the truth. There's a house up here on the right." He points around a blind curve. "Not sure it made it through the storm, but there's a family living there."

Or they were living there. It's destroyed. The only thing letting us know a house once stood there is the concrete block foundation. I'm not even sure how that withstood the ferocity of the wind and storm surge, but it did.

"Let's go look and see what we got." He puts the SUV in park.

Silently we both get out, putting gloves on. Neither one of us want to find someone here. It's the unspoken prayer between the both of us. I've seen dead bodies before, but I don't want to see one that's been here for over a week in the temps we've been dealing with.

"I'll take this section" – I point to a post that sticks up – "and sweep to the left, if you wanna take the rest."

He nods and together, we get to work. It takes longer than I realized it would, because it's hard to see under all the rubble. We have to physically move pieces, calling out for survivors. This wasn't what I imagined when I signed up for this job, but life doesn't always work out the way we envision it. That's one of the most important lessons I've learned. One I'll never forget.

Hours later, we've combed the entire wreckage; luckily we didn't find anyone. One time I thought maybe I had and a scream had lodged in my throat. I couldn't articulate what I was feeling, but then I realized it wasn't what my brain had convinced me it was. Instead of being a body, it was a doll. Sullivan goes back to the SUV, pulling a spray can of paint out.

"Come help me prop this up." He points to a piece of plywood the occupants probably put up to protect them from the elements. Looking at it lying there, I try to think about what they went through the night this storm went through. We were lucky, in a hotel set up for us, not necessarily worrying about our safety, but how did this family feel? Were they in the house when it collapsed? Did they take refuge in a closet, knowing it was coming down around them? If I could save anyone from going through terror like that, I would.

When we have it so that anyone can see it from the road, he takes the can and sprays a circle with an "x" along with the date to let people who come after us know that it's already been checked.

"There's four more houses on this road. You okay to help me check them?"

"Whatever you need help with, I'm here for."

We get into the SUV and as he cranks up the air conditioning, he looks over at me. "You're a good dude, Cutter. Thanks for coming and helping us. We've had help over the years and some people come up in here acting like they're better than we are because they've offered to help. You've actually shown up and been helpful. Thank you."

"No need to thank me, I've learned a lot in the short time I've been here. I feel like it should be me thanking you."

He reaches out, shaking my hand. "Glad you're here."

I realize as we drive farther up the road, looking out to see if there are any other people who've got left behind, I'm glad I'm here too.

CHAPTER TWELVE

Rowan

AFTER THE LAST week of work, it's nice to not wake up to an alarm. When I finally get my eyes open, I realize how nice it actually is this morning. After Cutter left, I laid in bed, thinking about him probably much more than I should have. In fact, I know it was more than I should have.

Rolling over, I pick up my phone, gasping loudly when I see it's past two in the afternoon. I obviously needed the rest, but it's been a very long time since I slept that late.

My stomach growls, reminding me of how long it's been since I ate. An idea pops into my head, and I fire off a text.

R: Hey bro, you had lunch yet?

I'm surprised when he answers right back.

S: Not yet, you wanna meet me? I haven't seen much of you lately.

My eyes roll. Since everything that happened, he's beyond protective. Almost suffocating at times, but I know I'm lucky. If I didn't have him, I don't know if I would still be alive, and that's as honest as I can be about how far I've come.

Sulllivan and I have always been closer than me and Braylon. Someday I hope that changes, but Sullivan has always been there for me, and never judged me.

R: Would love to. You pick.
S: The sandwich shop?
R: How did I know you'd say that?
S: Screw you.

I laugh loudly. There's a woman there he's been interested in for years. She drags him along, letting him think they might one day have a shot, but I know. I can tell by looking at her, she's not interested. It's not even about him, it's about her, but I wish she'd let him go. She knows what he wants, and yet keeps him tethered to her.

R: When do you get lunch?
S: An hour? Is that good for you?
R: Yeah, I'll meet you there.
S: Cutter's riding with me today. We'll see you soon.

Now why in the hell did he have to say that. Something

that was going to be low-key and fun with my older brother is now going to give me anxiety. What do I wear? Do I put on makeup? What should I do with my hair? All questions I haven't asked myself in years.

Who is this Rowan?

I don't recognize her, but I can say I like her.

With a small noise of excitement, I hop out of the bed and run for my bathroom. With any luck I'll have just enough time to look decent.

I HATE MY BROTHER, along with the smug smile across his face as I park next to where he and Cutter stand next to the SUV. If looks could kill, he'd be dead. His eyebrows raise, and I want to slap them down. He knows exactly what he's doing.

"How are you two?" I ask as I get out and face them.

"It's been a long day," Sullivan answers for them. "We've been searching the outskirts." He mentions the name many locals call a group of little more than shanties around the outer edges of town.

"Find anything?" Honestly, I don't really want to know, but sometimes it helps other first responders to talk about it.

"No," Cutter answers for the two of them.

"Thank God."

I can only imagine what it would look like, how it would feel. In our line of work we see so much destruction, so many lives torn apart. For once it's nice to hear something went right.

"After you." Sullivan opens the door, gesturing both me and Cutter inside.

I'm hit with the smell of freshly baked bread. In all honesty, this is one of my favorite hole-in-wall places to eat. I just hate how Sullivan gets his hopes up every time we're here.

"If it's not my two favorite public servants." Candice, the girl who holds Sullivan's heart in her hands, waves as we enter. "To what do I owe this pleasure?"

"We're hungry." He bellies up to the cold case like it's a bar.

As the two of them do their talking and flirting action, I turn to Cutter. "I'm glad you didn't find anything out there today."

"Me too, judging by the way the buildings were completely demolished, it wouldn't have been good if we did."

We're quiet for a few moments, waiting for Sullivan to stop flirting. When it looks like it's going to take longer than I imagined, I turn to Cutter again. "I had fun with you last night."

He smiles, a dimple popping on his left cheek. "I had fun with you too. We should do it again sometime."

"We should." I nod.

God, this is embarrassing and painful. I've lost the ability to flirt.

"Poking the bear, I see." He gestures to my chest.

It's then I realize I'm wearing an Auburn shirt. I laugh loudly. "Didn't even think about it."

"Can we take a selfie?" he asks. "I want to send this to my sister-in-law who bleeds 'Bama crimson. I need to know how she'll react. Her and her mom have season tickets."

"Sure." I push my glasses more securely up onto my nose.

"You don't know what you're saying sure to, but I like your adventurous spirit."

My spirit has never been adventurous, but I let him have this. He turns into me, putting his arm around my neck, pulling me into his side. Even after a long day of working in what I know were hot temperatures he still smells good. It's also hard not to notice how perfectly I fit into the crook of his body. He holds his phone out, pressing his cheek to mine.

"Smile."

His voice is so deep in my ear. It makes me think of other reasons for his voice to be that deep and that close to me.

"Thank you." He pulls back too quickly. "Thank you so much."

I'm left bereft and cold where our bodies were touching. "No problem."

He fires off a text, and I have an idea. "Can you text it to me too?"

It's a way to ask for his number without really asking for it. It's crazy how hard I give myself a pat on the back for it.

"Sure." He gives me a grin. It almost says I know what you're doing, but right now I don't even care. I fire off my number to him, and blatantly save his when I get the picture.

It's not a minute later when Cutter's phone comes through with a FaceTime request. He laughs loudly. "Oh, this should be good."

He answers it. "Hey, Stelle."

"Don't hey Stelle me, how can you be standing with your arm around someone wearing an Auburn shirt? You just wait until I show my mother and my husband. How could you even speak to your nephew when you're a traitor?"

He laughs even louder. "The same way I'm speaking to

you. Stella, meet Rowan, she's been helping us while we've been here. She's a fellow first responder."

He turns the phone to where I am, and I can almost see this beautiful woman grinding her teeth. "Hi." She waves, holding a cute toddler in her arms. They're both wearing Alabama shirts. I do my best not to let the disgust show on my face. "We're a Roll Tide family around here, sorry I reacted so badly."

"No problem, I get it. I mean, we'll win the Iron Bowl, but you can have your little Rammer Jammer. It's cute."

She makes a face, and then it turns into a smile. "I like you, you'll be good for him."

The way she says those words startle me, and I give the phone back to him. Their conversation plays in my periphery just like Sullivan and Candace's does. Will this ever be the way my life works out?

When everyone is finally finished with their conversations and flirting, we take a seat and order. But the lightheartedness I felt earlier is gone. I can't explain, couldn't even if I wanted to, but sometimes little moments in life trigger me. They make me think about what could have been. What I had and what I lost.

"You okay?" Sullivan asks as we get situated in our booth.

"Fine." I give him the smile I always do when something is bothering me and I don't want to talk about it. "Tell me more about your plans for the rest of the day."

He talks, just like I want him to, but I don't listen. The words are all jumbled as I try to make sense of what's going on inside my brain and my heart. Emotions are warring with one another. There's no doubt in my mind I want to move forward, I want to be the type of person who can accept the type of love I deserve, but I've held myself back for so long, I'm unsure of how to let it back into my life.

The door to the shop dings and in walks a family. A little girl who would be the age of my daughter now, along with what looks like her mom and dad. I watch them, wondering how differently my life would be right now if I hadn't lost her.

But for the first time I don't feel the loss as acutely as I have for so long. My gaze goes across the table to where Cutter sits. If I hadn't lost her, I probably wouldn't be in this position right now, and I may not have met him.

Good things come to those who wait is what I've always been told, and as I watch him take a bit of the sandwich he ordered, I wonder if my patience is paying off.

Is it finally my turn?

CHAPTER THIRTEEN

Cutter

MY PHONE VIBRATES in my pocket, and I grin seeing my mom's smiling face.

L: Auburn fan huh?
C: Jesus. Christ. That quick?
L: Whitney already came into The Café. Stella told her about this girl with the Auburn shirt on. Whit said well at least we still got Ransom. You've been withdrawn as a member of the family.
C: That's okay
L: Cutter, seriously?
C: This girl, Mom, I think she's worth it.
L: I love you, Cutter. Be safe.
C: I will, love you too.

As soon as I'm done, my phone vibrates again.

R: Hope your ass knows I'm in the doghouse because of you. Rambo and I are sleeping on the fucking couch tonight.
C: Why?
R: Duh, does Little Ms. Auburn ring a bell.
C: Shut the fuck up.
R: You know my wife is serious about football.
C: Let me go cry you a river.
R: Dammit Cutter, I gotta go, but you'll pay for this.

"Why are you so popular tonight?" Tucker looks over at me.

"Stella's big mouth told everybody I'm dating an Auburn fan. It's all-out war now."

"Good luck with all of that," Tucker laughs as he answers his own phone. Probably his nightly phone call from Karsyn.

I DON'T KNOW why I'm here, standing in front of Rowan's apartment. I saw her this afternoon, but I want to see her again. Sitting in the hotel room, listening to Tucker talk to Karsyn, it reminded me of what I don't have. I'm acutely aware of what I want, and more than anything, it gave me an overwhelming urge to see Rowan again.

Knocking on the door, I feel like I'm about to go on my

first date. My stomach is in my throat, and my hands fucking shake.

When she opens the door, the surprise is evident in the way she takes a step back, but then a smile curls at the tips of her lips. "Cutter?"

"Hey." I reach back, scratching my neck, before I start playing with the necklace I wear.

"Hey," she answers. Glancing down at her, I see she's changed into a tank top and short shorts. Her feet are bare, toenails painted a hot pink color I wouldn't have imagined she'd wear. I'd expect it on say Stella or Karsyn, but not on this woman who hides so much from the outside world. "What are you doing here, Cutter?

That's a great question, one I asked myself the entire time I was on my way to her. I wondered how I'd answer when she asked, because I knew she would ask. "I just wanted to see you."

She grins, looking down bashfully. "Really? You saw me this afternoon."

"It wasn't nearly enough."

Fuck it, if there's anything my time here has taught me, it's that tomorrow isn't promised and you've got to do the things you want while you can.

"Cutter..."

"Walk with me?" I beg her. We're blocks from the beach. "Please, walk with me."

The indecision slides across her face, but then I can tell the minute she makes the decision. Will it be one that changes both our lives? We won't know until years from now, but I'm triumphant. All I want to do is get to know her better.

"Okay, be right back."

It feels like an eternity as I wait for her, but she returns soon enough carrying a blanket.

"Just in case we get sick of walking."

She shuts her door, and that's when I notice she has a keypad along with a traditional keyhole for a lock. "This is such an awesome thing for when I don't want to carry my keys. Like right now."

Like the gentleman my mom raised me to be, I grab the blanket.

"Thanks for agreeing to come with me."

She shrugs. "It's a nice night, and I haven't been for a walk on the beach in a long time."

I hope that means she hasn't been out on a date in a long time, I don't want to compete with someone else for her, but I will if I have to.

We walk in a comfortable silence, not like the one we had at lunch today. When we get to the road crossing, I reach down, grabbing her hand without even thinking about it. She gasps when our skin connects.

"Is this okay?" I hold up our entwined fingers.

"Yeah." She licks her lips. "It's okay."

She feels it, that magnetic electricity I feel. She must, it's so palpable between the two of us. If we're lucky it'll ignite one day, but if we aren't careful it'll burn bright and fizzle out like an electric storm before we've been able to really experience it. The butterflies in my stomach push me to make a move tonight.

There's a heaviness to the air, like our attraction is hanging between us. One of us needs to make a move on it, and if it has to be me, then I will.

The beach is empty, much like I expected it to be this

time of night. We walk next to the shoreline, dipping our toes in the still-warm waters of the gulf.

"Do you worry about your brothers being cops?" I ask her, not yet having let go of our hand.

"Oh yeah." She nods. "Every time we get a call about it being an officer when either one of them are on duty, I never feel okay until we get there and I see it's not them. How about you?"

"Scares the shit out of me. Especially now that Ransom has a family. He got shot on duty a few years ago, and we were all worried. He and Stelle, they were dating but they didn't let anyone in on the secret, because they were afraid if they broke up it would divide our friends group and families. Looking at them now, though, I don't know how any of us didn't see that they were together. He loves his wife and kid more than anything in this world. I know he'll fight to come home to his family every night, but sometimes..." I shake my head. "Like we see the worst in people, ya know? More than anyone else, we know that some human beings don't respect life. They give no shits that these other people have families to go home to. I worry a lot about Keegan growing up without a dad, Stella having to bury her husband. I think that's why I stay so close. Stella's got a brother, but there's just a part of me that feels like no one would take care of them if something happened the way I would. I know how Ransom loves them, I know how much he loves them. Maybe it's weird..."

"No," she answers. "I get it."

We're a bit quiet as we walk farther down the beach. She lets go of my hand and runs a little ahead of me so that we're facing one another.

"You're a good guy, Cutter."

The moonlight is behind her, giving her a glow. She looks like a goddess bathed in the most sensual light I've ever seen. "Not so much right now," I admit. "Not the way I'm thinking about you."

"What would you say if I told you I'm thinking about you the same way."

I lick my lips, letting my eyes drift down to hers. "Can't be the way I'm thinking about you, sweetheart."

"Yeah it can be," she counters.

"Oh yeah?"

"Yeah."

My heart pounds and I clench my hands into fists at my sides. "Show me, Ro. Show me how you're thinking of me."

She reaches up, pulling the holder she has in her hair down, throwing it on the ground. The large mass of darkness I've wanted to see since the first moment I saw her is unleashed, and before I know it, she's running to me.

I catch her in my arms, hands immediately going to her ass as she wraps her legs around my waist. Our lips attack one another, taking the kiss I've wanted for far too long. We fit together, our tongues jockeying for position. She's small against me, so much smaller than I expected her to be.

Somehow I get us to the sand. "Wait, wait." I break our mouths apart. "Let's use the blanket."

In a matter of seconds I have both it and her spread out before me. "Are you still okay with this?"

I'm worried that cooler heads will have prevailed and maybe she's decided it was the moonlight and the chemistry between us that caused her to jump me. When she opens her arms to me again, I want to shout to the world how lucky I am.

My body covers hers, settling into the cradle of her

thighs. Our mouths take one another, our tongues entwine, and our bodies rub together. I put one hand onto the blanket so I can lever myself up slightly from where I'm pressed against her. Her hand comes up to mine, holding onto my wrist, and she adjusts so that her neck opens up completely to me.

"Hmmm," she moans when my tongue tastes the tendons of her throat. "God, Cutter." Her words make my cock punch against the fabric of my shorts.

My other hand tips her chin, giving me more room to work against the flesh of her neck, her earlobes, and then partially down her chest. When I can't breathe any longer, I lift up slightly on my knees, looking at my handiwork.

Her nipples are peaked against the fabric of her shirt. Reaching down, I palm her tits, brushing the peaks against my palms, then squeezing hard as I dare. We're new to each other and I don't know how she likes it yet.

Her arms go up, tangling in her hair, as she thrusts toward me. "Yes," she moans.

Oh, so it's like that, huh?

Reaching down, I grasp the edge of her tank top, pulling it down so that it's just below where the edge of her bra is. White skin contrasts against a teal colored bra, edges of lace cup the globes I want so badly to get a look at.

"Please." She thrusts up into my touch again.

Without hesitation, I pull the lace edges of the bra away from her skin, moaning when I see two tight peaks reaching up toward me, begging for attention. The moon gives off enough light that I can see they're dark with desire.

Leaning down, I blow on one, chuckling when she makes a noise of frustration in her throat. She tangles her fingers into my hair, pulling me to where she wants me.

Complying with her unspoken demand is one of the best things I've ever done. I'm convinced of it. My tongue circles the bud, before I close my lips around it and suck.

"Harder!"

I'm great at taking direction, especially when a woman is telling me how to pleasure her. I use my teeth to slightly score the flesh before I bathe it in my saliva again, running my tongue around it.

Her hands press on my ass cheeks, and my cock finds right where it wants to be. Grinding against each other in the moonlight, we chase the pleasure we've both been denying between us for so long.

CHAPTER FOURTEEN

Rowan

WILD.

Uninhibited.

Selfish.

These are words I would never have used to describe myself before this moment, but right here with Cutter? I feel them all. Wild because I'm on a public beach, even if it is after the sun has gone down. Uninhibited because I'm moaning loudly, letting him know I love what he's doing to my body. Selfish because I want this so much.

The old Rowan wouldn't even be here right now, much less letting a man do these things to her.

"Don't stop," I beg, tilting my head back.

Moisture hits me on the forehead, once, twice. It takes me a few seconds to realize it's raining. Cutter pulls back, his green eyes roving my face. He's panting, the skin of his chest pressing against mine. "Do you want to go back to your apartment?"

I know myself well enough to realize how rare this moment truly is. As soon as we get up from here and we go back to my apartment, this will be over. I'm not ready for it to be over. We're just getting started.

"No." I grip his hair with my fingers. "Keep going."

"Are you sure about this?"

"I've never been more sure of anything in my entire life."

Cutter is a man on a mission as he goes back to work on my body. His confident fingers take care of the shirt covering my torso, throwing it beside us. Those same fingers unbutton my shorts, shoving his hand in between the denim and the lace of my underwear. When he touches my clit, I scream.

"It's been so, so long." I grasp his hair tighter. "My God." I grind against him. "Please let me come, please give me one that I don't give myself."

He adjusts himself so that he's lying to the side of me. His mouth working the bare flesh of my breast, his fingers working the enflamed flesh between my thighs. I hold him tightly to me, almost like I'm afraid he'll get up and leave me.

So much has left in my short time here on earth. Right now I want this for me. If I'm doomed to a life of living without my daughter, then at least give me this night to help me make it through. A memory I can cling to that doesn't revolve around the worst night of my life.

Cutter is good at this, better than I gave him credit for. I can already feel myself flying, but it's so fast. I reach down, grabbing hold of his wrist, pressing it tightly to my core while at the same time trying to pull it away.

"Which do you want, baby?" He pulls away, voice deep with arousal.

Hearing him call me baby, God, I never thought I'd have anyone call me a pet name again. It flows right through me, sparking a longing that threatens to overtake me. It pushes the walls I've had built around my heart down and aside, allowing him to come over, under, or through them. I've not let anyone see who I am since the accident. Cutter is the only person who's been strong enough to do what I've needed.

"I don't know," I pant, wanting him to take what he knows I need.

"Yes you do," he encourages. "You know exactly what you want. Go for it. I'll give you anything you need."

And I know he will, if there's one thing I've come to learn about this man - it's he'll do anything he can to make others happy. Making the decision, I grab his hand this time holding it tightly to the nub that needs him so much.

"Yes," he praises. "Ride my hand baby, take whatever you need. Ride it."

I press up into him wanting to do exactly as he wants me to. Spreading my legs, I give myself over to him. Finally, I let down my guard and trust him to give me what I need. It doesn't take long until I'm there, body tightening, legs starting to close.

"You're so wet." Cutter nips at my tits again, using his teeth. The bite into my skin seems to be tethered to my pussy. Each time he nips, I feel a clench I haven't felt in a long time. "So fucking wet. I know it won't be tonight, but I can't wait to get my cock inside this pussy. Can't wait to press into you, feel you squeeze me. See you with your hair down and watch you ride me naked, full of confidence. You'll grind these hips against me, won't you? Press your clit down so I can make you feel good?"

I'm barreling head-first into the best orgasm of my life when he adds another finger to the mix between my thighs and the game is over. I come in a rush of wetness and emotions against his hand, my heart thumping a mile a minute and bright lights hiding my vision.

Cutter

FUCK, she's beautiful when she comes. I wonder if anyone's ever told her that. If I had my wits about me, I would, but she's blown my damn mind. All I can think about is the cock pressing tightly against my shorts.

Withdrawing my hand from between her thighs, I moan when she makes a noise of disappointment. Falling flat on my back, I do my best to try and deal with what just happened between us.

Reaching down, I palm my cock, working to get it out of my shorts. Once it's free of the zipper, I make a noise of relief.

She looks over at me, her blue eyes smoldering an almost black, making it hard to see in the moonlight.

"Don't worry about me, that was for you."

"No." She gives me a half-smile, coming up on her knees.

The Rowan I thought I knew has turned into a vixen. She grabs my length in her hand, using her palm to stroke it up and down. "This." She looks down. "This is for me."

I'm not prepared, not even a little bit when she leans over, taking me into her throat. An oath rips its way out of my chest, my hands go to her hair, guiding her up and down.

"Your mouth..." My eyes drift closed as I press up between her lips. "So wet, so fuckin' warm, my God."

Not to be an ass, but I've had my fair share of blow jobs. Being a football player will do that for you, but this one ranks right at the very top. I don't know why, don't want to dissect anything that's going on right now between us, but I know she's blowing my fucking mind.

"Can you take me deeper?" I whisper, holding onto the top of her head.

She glances up at me, my dick in her mouth, and nods.

Hottest. Thing. Ever.

In increments neither one of us can barely stand, I press between her lips, not wanting to overwhelm her, or myself. Honest to God, I'm already about to blow, and it's beyond pitiful. Her gag reflex stops her when I get almost all the way in.

"Breathe through your nose," I coach, punching my head back against the blanket when she listens and takes me deeper. "Fuck, Rowan." I don't know how I'm going to survive this, how I'm going to look at this woman in everyday situations and not see her how she is right now. A siren sucking my cock.

Just when I don't think it can get any better, she speeds up, and I know it's the end for me. Gripping her hair, I do my best to pull her back, but she refuses. She fights against me, obviously wanting what she wants, and who am I to stop her?

"Gonna come, gonna come, gonna come," I warn her.

But she doesn't stop, she doesn't pull back. The only thing she does is work faster, harder, and that's the end for me.

I come in a rush I haven't felt since I was a teenager getting my first hand job. She takes it, swallowing it with an enthusiasm I didn't expect. It's just another thing that throws me off my game. Another surprise lurking behind the exterior of a woman who doesn't know how to let her hair down.

She pulls back, wiping her mouth with her fingers.

"How many people know this about you," I ask in a guttural voice.

"Know what?" She smirks.

"You know what. Who else knows how talented and passionate you are? Who else knows you're a lady in the street and a freak between the sheets?"

She giggles loudly. "Nobody."

I scrutinize her. She must be lying. Nobody hides that kind of talent. "Surely somebody."

"Nope." She lays next to me, sighing heavily. "I haven't had anybody in my life for a long time, and the person I had before..." She stops, playing with a ring on her finger. "Let's just say there was too much bad blood between us for me to want to do anything like that for him."

Now I'm curious, but I know she has to come to me on her own.

"Well, regardless, thank you for letting me be the person you decided to give your gift to."

She laughs again, while I reach over and grab her hand. The rain is still coming down, misting slightly and as we lay there looking at the stars, I can't help but wonder if there's ever been a more serene time in my life.

CHAPTER FIFTEEN

Cutter

"WHY ARE YOU SO HAPPY TODAY?"

Tucker's voice is full of annoyance when he hears me whistling. We're taking a drive through Paradise Lost, looking to see if there are any more places that need to be cleared. If all goes well, the LSERT will be packing up and moving out this weekend. I'm not sure at all how I feel about leaving Rowan, but I can't deny I'm happy today.

More relaxed than I've been in what feels like years. "Just happy. What's it to you? Don't come raining on my happiness parade."

"Sorry," he sighs. "I miss the hell out of Karsyn. By this time they should have relieved us, but since we're coming home this weekend, we're staying longer than normal. It's not something I really planned on."

I kind of want to tell him no one plans on a hurricane, but I figure my opinion isn't what he wants right now. "It's funny." I reach over, scratching Major. "When we came down here, I came because I didn't have anything else going on. I didn't have anything besides family to keep me tied to Laurel Springs. Now, I'm not sure I wanna go back," I admit.

"She got to you that much?"

"She has."

Especially last night, seeing her come out of her shell and being real with me? I wasn't sure I'd ever see her like that. Now that I've had a little taste of it, I don't want to give it up. More than anything I hope I'm the man she feels at ease with all the time.

"I get it." Tucker looks over at me. "When I realized Karsyn was it for me, I would have done anything she asked to get her back."

Chuckling, I lock eyes with him. "The difference between you and me is that I'm not stupid enough to let her go."

"You don't necessarily let them go, sometimes you have to let them fly. And when I say them, I mean us too, the ones who think we've done the wrong thing, or right thing, no matter how misguided it is. People are broken, Cutter. All of us are. I am, you are, she is. When we fly away broken, we come back whole, put together by the experiences we had. Everyone has a hill to climb, nothing in life is easy. You know that more than most, but one of the worst things you can do is assume letting someone go is stupid. It can be a necessity."

Immediately I'm taken back to what she said about her and the other person who may have known about her oral skills. Them having bad blood. Could it be she's broken, like Tucker said, and I'm just a piece of the glue she's thinking about using to put herself back together again?

The thought leaves a bad taste in my mouth, if I'm being honest. I always told myself after what happened in

Tuscaloosa, I wouldn't be the person who hung around with one woman until I was sure I could see a life with her. Lord have I lived up to it. One-night stands, week-long flings - those have been the name of the game for me. If I were asked why Rowan seems different, I can't name one thing. It would be everything.

Highly emotional meet-up? Oh yeah, the hurricane definitely moved things along.

Attraction? We've got that in spades.

Chemistry? Thinking about her right now is giving me wood.

But there's something that makes the back of my neck itch. We don't know much about each other on the inside. What we do seem to know is slightly superficial. I get the feeling she holds parts of herself back, and it's imperative I know what those parts are.

"I think I understand what you're saying." I rub Major's head absent-mindedly.

"Do you?"

"She and I, we haven't had the deep conversations, we've scratched the surface, but nothing has gone iceberg level."

"Iceberg level?" He makes a noise in his throat.

"Yeah, how you can see a little bit sticking out of the water, but there's years and years of bad habits and decisions below the surface? Ya know, iceberg level."

"That's an interesting way of putting it."

Truth be told it's the analogy most like my life. I let everybody see that tiny little bit above the water. The mass they can run into and be stopped, but underneath? Nobody's seen that for a very long time, and I realize I have a decision to make too. Am I willing to let her in? Am I willing to tell her about Tuscaloosa? Lay myself bare and let her see the worst days I had, how I thought my young heart would never heal?

I'm willing to tell her, just not right now.

Not when our time together might be so short. Who knows what's going to happen in the next few days. We don't even know if we'll be seeing each other after I leave.

My chest tightens as I think about not seeing her again. Blowing out a deep breath, I try to not let the heaviness of the conversation bring me down, especially when we turn a curve and find a tree across the road.

"I thought the department of transportation had taken care of all of these."

Tucker groans. "I did too, and I don't know what's in this SUV as far as saws go. Wonder if anybody's been down this road?"

"I hope so, if there are people living here and nobody has, they've been left alone for a long time."

Immediately the adrenaline surge I get when things start to happen rushes through me. My hands slightly shake as I get out of the SUV and run to the back. Popping the trunk, I search for the chainsaw most of these are equipped with. Tucker's got Major out, and they're going over to where the tree is across the road, presumably trying to see if there's a way around it.

"It's completely blocking," Tucker yells. "We've got to find a way to make a cut. I think I can see what looks like a driveway."

How he can see, I'm not sure, but I believe him. Tucker's one of the best, and if he says we need to try and get through this, then we need to do it yesterday.

Finding the only saw that's back there, along with some

gloves, I grab them up, running over to where Tucker and Major stand.

"This is the skinniest part of the tree I can see. If we can at least make a spot for us to walk through, we can get back there and see if anyone needs help."

His logic is sound. "You want me to do the cutting, or do you?"

"I'll do it." He gives me Major's leash, and takes the saw from my hands.

As we watch, I can't help but think we need to get this done quickly, a feeling in my gut tells me someone needs our help, and they need it fast.

I just hope we can get to them in time.

IT TAKES us an hour to get through the tree, and as soon as we have a clear path, I take off at a run, needing to be somewhere.

Where?

I don't know.

I just know I need to be there.

"There's the driveway I saw." Tucker points to the left, indicating what could be a driveway. Right now though, it just looks like a gravel, rutted, mess, probably from the hurricane and torrential downpours.

Running up the driveway, we make as much noise as we can to alert whoever may be living there.

"Hello!"

"Do you need help?"

"Is anyone here?"

That's when we hear someone screaming. "Please help! My wife's in labor. Please help us."

We look at each other, knowing there was a reason we had to come down this road. I kick my speed into high gear, similar to how fast I would run when playing football. When I get to the front porch, he's holding the door open.

"She's been in labor the past fifteen hours, but I think she's ready to push and I have no idea what to do."

"Don't panic." I look back at Tucker. "Go to the SUV and get my go bag. There's a few things we can use in it, but you better call for an ambulance, that way we can get them to the hospital ASAP."

"Got it."

Major whines, looking between the two of us, not sure what he should do. He's bonded so significantly with Karsyn, I think seeing this woman in pain is bothering him.

"Go with Tuck," I tell him. "We'll be fine here."

He barks, then turns around, leaving me alone with these people I don't know. It's not the first time I've been in a situation like this, more than likely won't be the last.

"When did your water break?"

"Yesterday," the woman pants.

She's sweating, they don't have power back yet here, and the only way I can see is a lantern they've lit in the room they're in. "Are there windows in here?"

"Just beyond those curtains," the husband says.

"Take them down so we'll be able to see. I need to check how far along she is, and the more light I have the better."

When the light from outside exposes what's happening, my stomach drops, there's much more blood than there should be, and I'm scared this mother and baby may not make it.

CHAPTER SIXTEEN

Rowan

"DID SOMETHING HAPPEN TO YOU?" Isaac asks, looking me up and down. "Get your hair cut or change your glasses?" He looks completely puzzled.

"No, why?" I laugh.

"You look different today."

"Different good, or different bad?"

He tilts his head to the side. "Different good. You look more alive than I've probably seen you look in years."

Part of me wants to tell him it's because of Cutter. All because of what we experienced together last night. Another part of me wants to keep it a secret. Like if I don't tell anyone, it can never go away. I have a real fear it'll go away. Nothing good in my life has stayed the same since I lost her.

"You haven't let yourself be happy in a long time, Ro. I think it's okay to allow yourself whatever it is you're doing."

Isaac knows. The way he quirks the side of his mouth is a giveaway. Not that I wouldn't eventually tell him. To be partners, you have to trust the person you ride with implicitly. And I trust him more than I've trusted half the people in my life.

"Is it though?" I question. "I've stopped asking myself what can go wrong, because so much can."

"Everybody has shit that goes wrong, Ro. It's how you bounce back that matters."

A snort comes out of my nose. "Then I must be the slowest person in the world to bounce back."

"There's not a time limit on it."

"I love you for being nice to me." I wink at him. "You're doing your best to keep my pride intact."

"Hey." He looks over, as we finish up stocking our ambulance. "You've had to live through a lot. Most people will never have to deal with one-tenth of what you've dealt with. You're allowed to take some time, no matter how long that time is. Nobody knows how we're going to grieve. Especially not when we lose our children."

His kind words bring tears to my eyes.

For months I've heard the whispers, people saying I should be living my life, not living in the shadow of Etta. Named after my favorite jazz singer. Being near New Orleans, I've always been a fan, even if it makes me feel like I'm from another time period. They've whispered I should get back out there, give my ex-husband another shot.

They all think they know what happened, assume he's repented. He's a changed man, they whisper, but they don't know the depths to which I was hurt. What I suffered that day. The one person who was supposed to be my rock to lean on. He'd stood by as I struggled to save her life, as I worked and worked to get her heart going again.

Truth be told, I'm not sure I'll ever be able to forgive him.

Isaac looks like he wants to say something, but we're interrupted by the radio going off. We listen intently.

"Did I hear what I think I just heard?" I glance at him.

He looks back at me, disbelief across his face. "I think so. Tucker and Cutter are delivering a baby."

"Let's go!" I'm already scrambling to my seat in the passenger side of the ambulance, ready to go as Isaac takes the driver's seat.

When he turns on the lights and siren, my adrenaline automatically flows. It's like some sort of conditioning I've become accustomed to. As soon as I hear those sounds, I immediately prepare myself for whatever may happen. It's one of the only ways I've been able to do this job.

Within minutes we're on the road they've radioed in they were at. Then we encounter the tree.

Of course the notch they made to go through isn't big enough for our ambulance, it's barely big enough for a stretcher. "You think we can carry it?"

He looks at me, and I know he's seeing me for the less imposing figure I make, but I'm strong.

"I don't know, Ro."

"I can do this."

"It's really heavy."

"Don't take it easy on me because I'm a woman, don't think less of me. I can do what I need to so we can get the job done."

"I don't doubt you, I just don't want you to hurt yourself."

Anger and frustration fly all over me. "If I were a man would you be worried?"

He shuts his mouth quickly. "Point taken, but just know, if you can't do this - if you're uncomfortable, I have it and I won't think less of you."

While I appreciate what he's saying, it doesn't make me feel much better. He runs to the back of the rig, grabbing out what he thinks we may need. We fold up the stretcher, each taking an end.

And together, we make the march to the house. Hoping we get there in time. Knowing there's a real possibility we won't. Before we get far enough down the driveway to see the house, we can hear her screaming.

"She must be close," I tell Isaac and the two of us pick up our pace.

My arms are burning, my legs are on fire. He was right, this is heavy for me. Too heavy, but I won't admit it. Not when someone needs my help as much as this woman sounds like she needs it.

We get to the porch, Tucker and Major meeting us. "Thank God you're here. Cutter's got her in the bedroom, there's a lot of blood."

My stomach drops. I've never lost a patient before. We've had to declare a few deceased, but they were already gone by the time we got there. In those cases there are no life-saving measures we can do. But every patient I've ever had has been alive when we got them to the hospital.

I decide here and now, this one will be too. Both her *and* the baby. Nothing else will do. We get to the bedroom and I see the blood Tucker was talking about. Immediately we drop the stretcher and glove up.

"What's happening?" I ask Cutter as I take up the spot next to his shoulder.

"I think she's got a placental abruption," he whispers. "I

also think this baby is big and she's tired. I'm not sure we'll be able to deliver it."

Taking a look at the woman, she's pale, her eyes are closed, and she's very lethargic. "We can't do a c-section here."

"Right? We've gotta get her to the hospital and it'll take hours for us to cut that tree up."

"Then let's go." I look at Isaac, nodding at him. "We've got to move her."

Going up to her head, I put gloves on, and reach into my go bag for a cool pack. "How are you doing? What's your name, honey?"

"Anna." Her voice is tired, barely there and really starting to scare me. "Anna, we're gonna take care of you. When was your baby due?"

"Not for another three weeks," she moans as another contraction rips through her.

Which means Cutter's probably right in his assessment. "Okay, here's what we're going to do. I'm going to get an IV running for you, to give you some fluids while we get you to the main road. Hopefully it'll make you feel better."

She nods, but I'm unsure if she understands exactly what's going on. Cutter and Isaac get her moved over, and I work on getting the IV started. Tucker and Major go before us, clearing away branches that will impede the stretcher. "Here." I hand the IV bag to her husband. "You hold this up." And in a lower voice, I warn, "Tell her you love her, she needs to hear it."

He takes my unspoken fear and immediately begins talk to her, telling her about all the plans they've made for the baby and their family. How she's a fighter and she's going to make it through this.

In this moment, I do my best to separate from what's happening. If we get too close, sometimes we can't perform our jobs to the best of our abilities.

It feels like a year, but eventually we see our ambulance and the SUV Tucker and Cutter were riding in. The group of us pick up our pace because we know we're close.

Once we get her onto the ambulance, Isaac takes his spot up front, Cutter and I start taking care of her in the back. When we get her hooked up to monitors, both of us sigh. The baby is still alive.

"See this line?" I point to a squiggly line on a printout of paper. "That's your baby. We're gonna get you to the hospital and you're going to be fine."

She looks like she believes me, and I'm glad I'm able to say the right things for her. At least I don't feel as if I'm lying. Her heartbeat is strong, as is the baby's.

Cutter and I connect eyes over the stretcher, sharing a moment neither one of us probably thought we'd ever have. I smile at him, and he smiles back at me, proud that we were able to do this, thankful he knew what to do and lucky that God seemed to be on our side today.

Stories like this? These are exactly why I decided to go into this field, and I hope later on in life I can meet this family again and see just how much they've grown.

"It's a girl," the woman says. "We're gonna name her Tatum for the hurricane."

Both Cutter and I laugh.

"That seems right about perfect."

CHAPTER SEVENTEEN

Cutter

MY EYES WATCH Tucker as he's putting his things together. We don't leave until tomorrow afternoon, but here he is. Already getting his stuff packed. After the day we've had, I can't believe he's not experiencing the same kind of adrenaline crash I am.

"You're excited, huh?"

He smiles that stupid smile of dudes in love everywhere. "Yeah, I can't wait to see Syn, feel her wrapped in my arms, lay in bed with her. I miss every single thing about her. Even the shit I didn't think I would miss."

I wonder if this is how it's going to be for me, but obviously I'll be the complete opposite. I'm not going home to the woman I love. I'm leaving the one I'm growing to know, thinking I can see a future with. It's hard not to be excited for him, but it's hitting me that tonight might be the last night Rowan and I ever see each other. We haven't discussed what's going to happen when the LSERT leaves.

I guess we both thought we had more time. Tonight it's the one thing not on our side. I have to see her. It's not even a want, it's a need. A feeling deep in my bones, thudding against the wall of my chest, electricity running through my veins. If I don't see her now, I don't know what I'll do with myself.

"I'll be back."

"Going to see her?"

"Yeah, don't wait up."

He chuckles. "You ain't here tomorrow at two, I'm not waitin' on you. You can figure out your own way back to Laurel Springs."

"That's fair."

"More than," he argues.

"Yeah, yeah."

He throws something at me as I leave the room, but I duck in time for it to hit the door, instead of my head.

"Two o'clock, Cutter!"

"Got it."

But I really don't. It's hard to reconcile him being so excited to leave and me being so reluctant to let go. It's not at all what I had planned, and the epitome of everything I said I'd never be.

Going down to the truck we've been sharing since we got here, I get in, looking at the dashboard. There's a picture of Karsyn, smiling up at Tucker like he's her entire world. I'm man enough to admit I want it; I want every bit of what they have. Rowan's picture on my dashboard? That's right where it belongs.

The streets of Paradise Lost are closed this time of night. The only people out are the ones who desperately need something or the first responders. Seeing Sullivan at a stop light, I give him a wave.

He does the same back, and I wonder what he would think if he knew where I'm going, what I'm going to do? Would he be friendly or would he tell me to make sure I don't hurt Rowan? One thing I've learned is I can't live my life based on what other's think of me. So I choose to ignore what he may think.

The drive is quicker than I remember it being, almost as if I show up two seconds after I got in the truck. There's a light on in her window, and I wonder if she's sitting out on her balcony. Taking the stairs two at a time, I knock hurriedly, not wanting to waste a second of the time I'll be able to spend with her.

She comes to the door, carrying a bottle of Bud Light in her hand. "I hoped you'd be by tonight."

Aren't those the best fucking words I've ever heard? "Couldn't stay away."

"Come on in."

She opens the door wide enough for me to walk past her. "Are you drunk?" The way her eyes are heavy, the goofy smile on her face. I need to know.

"No, just feel really good. Sometimes it's hard for me to handle that crash, and today there was definitely a crash."

"Oh yeah." I follow her as she walks to her kitchen, grabbing me a bottle and handing it over. "Tucker's already packing in anticipation of leaving tomorrow, and I can't seem to sit still."

"I can't believe you're leaving tomorrow."

There's a sadness in her voice I've never heard before. It gives me hope that she's gonna miss me as much as I'm gonna miss her. "I know. It went way too fast. I wanted to spend my last night here with you."

Reaching over to me, she grabs my hand, walking us out to the balcony. "I'm glad." She turns around, a smirk on her face. "I wanted to spend your last night with you too."

At least we're on the same page. I follow her, noticing the sway of her hips, how they move back and forth with the intentional steps she's taking.

"I called the hospital," I tell her. "Mom and baby are doing just fine. I had to know. It didn't look so good when we arrived and I worried she wouldn't make it."

"Women giving birth are a lot stronger than you give them credit for," she laughs. "I know a thing or two about it."

The beer seems to have loosened her lips slightly. "Do you now?" I wonder what she means.

"I do, but that's a story for another time."

It makes me wish we had all the time in the world, but as of now, we only have hours. We each have a seat. When we get back out to the balcony.

"What do you want, Cutter?" she asks as we sit across from each other.

"You," I answer truthfully. "But it's not that simple. I want the real conversations. You know the ones that go into who we are as people and the shit we've been through. I want to know your darkest secrets and your dirtiest fantasies. Be the person you wake up to, and go to sleep at night beside."

Rowan opens her mouth, but no words come out. She closes it, then lifts her bottle to her lips, taking a healthy drink.

"Too much?"

I can be a little much for some, and now I'm scared I've pushed her away.

"No." She shakes her head, a smirk working its way across her mouth. "But how are we gonna do this? How are we gonna make it work?"

"Long distance. You come up to my apartment, I come down to yours, until we know for sure what we have. Eventually maybe one of us will change our address, you never know, but I want to explore time with you. I need to do it. I've never met anyone like you before."

She gets up, walking across from me to lean against the railing of the balcony. "I've never met anyone like you before either. Do you think you can handle me?"

Answering her smirk with one of mine, I nod. "I'm more than sure I can handle you, babe. You'll be putty in my hands."

She giggles. "You think so?"

"I know so."

"Big talk for a big man."

"If only you knew how big." I wink at her.

"Oh," she laughs. "I got a good idea the other night on the beach."

Our eyes lock in a stare of complete seriousness. It's as if the two of us know we're no longer playing. What's going to happen will change the trajectory of our relationship. Once we go this far we won't be able to go back.

"You sure?"

"Yeah." She's almost shy in her whisper, and I want to do nothing else but protect her. "I'm sure."

Those are all the words I need to get up, walk across the balcony, and take what I've wanted to take for hours: her mouth.

The two of us kiss hungrily, growling and moaning, fucking with our tongues, teeth clashing. Our hands fight against one another as we go for each other's clothing, trying to touch body parts hidden from anyone who might be able to see. I can't recall ever needing a woman as badly as I need this one.

"You're gonna ruin me," I tell her as I pull away. "I'm gonna think about you all the time, won't be able to get anything done. I'll just think about these past days and wonder why in the hell we weren't born in the same hometown so we can be near each other all the time."

"Maybe because we had to go through a lot of shit to appreciate each other."

Maybe she's right, but I'm done talking. Capturing her lips with mine, I show her what I want to do with her body, thrusting in and out slowly, pushing her chin this way and that, making sure to get every inch of her mouth in my kiss. The mouth that took me so far down her throat and swallowed every bit of the release I gave her.

Pulling back, I have to let her know. My thumb comes up to her lips, pulling them apart. "I love this mouth. Took my cum like a pro and knows exactly how much pressure to give when you're going down. I don't think I'll ever forget these lips, Ro."

"Good," she says before she takes my thumb in her mouth, circling her tongue around my nail, letting it go with a loud pop. "I want you to have something to think about when I'm not with you every day."

"Trust me." I shove my thumb back in, groaning when she circles it again. "You'll never have to worry about that. Pretty sure I have your lips imprinted on my dick."

CHAPTER EIGHTEEN

Rowan

GLANCING OVER AT CUTTER, I memorize his features. Unsure if we'll be able to make the long-distance thing work. I'm willing to give it a shot. What I'm *not* willing to do is let him leave here tonight without having him. If it's my only shot, I want to take it. *Have to* take it. It'll be something I regret for the rest of my life if I don't.

I already have enough regrets and what if's. I can't let this be another one. I'm standing against the railing of the balcony, smirking. He wants me, I can see it in his eyes, can tell by the way his body's tightened, the tent at the crotch of his shorts.

Everything says he wants me, and I want him just as badly. He slowly walks over to me, a swagger I've rarely seen in real life. Never thought I'd see walking toward me on a warm moonlit night in September on the Alabama coast, that's for damn sure. I grip the railing, using it to keep me from reaching out to him, and standing up.

"You're fuckin' beautiful."

The smell of Bud Light on his breath is as intoxicating as the smell I've come to associate with him. A musky, woodsy scent that's all man. Even if I didn't see him, I'd know him anywhere.

"You're not so bad yourself." I swallow roughly as his palm comes up to the side of my face, pushing the escaped tendrils of hair out of the way.

"Can I do it?"

"Do what?" My eyes drop to his lips, hooded so that they're only focused on the soft redness being pulled between his straight teeth.

"Take your hair down?"

"You do it for me," I move his hand up to where the clip holds the mass of my hair. "I trust you. Please."

He's careful, unbelievably careful when he reaches up and lets the clip go. The heavy mass falls down, past my shoulders, almost to my waist. Because of the weather today, it's slightly curly. Cutter runs his fingers through it, combing it back from my face.

"It's gorgeous."

"I haven't cut it in four years," I admit.

"Why not?"

I don't want to ruin this night, this moment. "I promise to tell you sometime soon, but not tonight. Tonight it's about us."

This answer seems to satisfy him. He tucks both hands against my scalp, palming it, using his forehead to tip my head back, exposing my neck to his lips. Keeping my eyes open, I look at the sky, wondering if we'll see the same stars when he's gone. Can I sit out here on this balcony, talk to him on the phone or through FaceTime and look at the same blanket of darkness he's looking at?

Yes, I decide. Yes, I can do this. Just because something isn't going to be easy doesn't mean I should give it up. Some things are meant to take longer, they're sweeter when you finally reach the point where you can enjoy them.

His mouth is ravishing my neck, so hard I know I'm going to have marks tomorrow. I want them, I crave them. I hold him to me tightly, not wanting to let him go.

Eventually my thighs work around his waist, holding on as best I can as he dominates my body. His mouth has moved down my neck, to the top of my chest. His nose pushes the edges of my tank top away, and I'm not wearing a bra tonight. The warm night air cups my bare skin, making my nipples peak for him.

"Mmmm," he moans when he sees my body react. "So tight."

They are tight, I can feel them pulling against my flesh. "Please," I beg. "They need you, I need you."

Doing this with Cutter is easy, easier than I thought it would be. Everyone told me, when it's easy don't let it go, but here I am - about to let him go. Running my hands down his neck, his back, and to his waist, I hold on tightly before dipping my fingers below the elastic band of his shorts. Cupping his ass, I hold him to me.

He lets my nipple go with a loud noise. "We should go inside. You deserve a comfortable bed."

I shake my head. "But it's not what I want, Cutter. I want wild, outside for the world to see, my hair sheltering us from prying eyes. I want everything I've never had before."

He moans deep in his throat. "God, you're perfect."

I've never been called perfect before. For him I want to be. Perfect for him, that is, not for anyone else.

He moves his hands down to my ass, palming them and bringing me backward into him. When eventually he takes a seat on my deck lounger, I straddle his waist.

"We know you can ride my hand." He smirks. "But can you ride my dick?"

I look down at him, admiring the way he's laid out before me, mine for the taking. "It's been a while, but I think I can remember how to do it."

He pushes his head back against the cushion, as he situates himself a little better. "I have no doubt I can show you if you need a refresher course."

"Do you have protection?" I ask him breathlessly. It's been so many years since I even thought about doing this anything I may have had is probably expired.

He jostles me, reaching into his back pocket, taking out his wallet. "I do, but I've only got one, so we better make this last."

There's a part of me that knows this won't last. We've been teasing each other for days and we're both ready. Reaching down, I grab his cock in my hand, rubbing the length up and down.

"Fuck," he hisses. "Don't make me come before I even get inside you."

The thought makes my nipples harden even further, to know I have as much control over this man as I do. I've never felt the heady possessiveness before. But with him, I know he's mine. There's no one else who's ever made me feel the way he does.

Standing up, I push my shorts and panties down, before reaching over to grab the condom out of his hand.

"Oh no." He pulls it out of my reach. "You put this on, and I sure as fuck won't make it inside of you. Let me do it."

I watch him with hungry eyes, taking in each experimental stroke he gives himself up and down. Reaching over with his free hand, he gently separates my thighs, using his pointer finger in a "come here" motion on my clit.

My knees almost give way as I feel and watch what he's doing. I'm not sure I can stand any longer when I finally reach down, grab his wrist, and do my best to pull him away. He's strong though, and resists for a split second longer.

"Put the rubber on and fuck me, Cutter."

His eyes darken with desire from the words.

"Yes, ma'am."

He does as I ask, pushing his shorts down, and pulling me over so that I'm straddling him again. There are no words as we get comfortable, before I reach back and grab his cock, holding it up as I slowly lower myself onto it.

"Goddamn," he groans, rolling his head around on the cushion. "You're so fuckin' tight. I'm not sure I won't blow three strokes into this."

"Fuck, I hope not," I admit, as I lower until he's deeply seated inside me.

Watching porn, using your fingers, and sex toys only do so much. They aren't red, hot-blooded male like Cutter and his dick. This right here is exactly what I've missed and as I start pushing up and coming down on his length, and I know it's not going to take me long either.

Especially when he moves his hand to the juncture of my thighs, rubbing my clit as he pushes up into me. Leaning forward, I grab hold of the metal frame of the chair, using it to help me move.

"Ohhhh God," I moan when he shoves me down and

presses up, going even deeper inside me. "Keep going, please don't stop."

"I won't." He presses his feet onto the chair, holding me up against his knees as I grind down on him, circling his thumb with the movement of my hips.

Throwing my head back, I don't even know what's happening as my tits bounce up and down with the motion of his thrusts. This is on some other plane I've never been on, some place where passion and satisfaction are guaranteed.

"I don't know how much longer I can hold off," he moans, speeding up the motion of his thumb.

"Me neither," I admit. "Stop holding back and go for it."

That's all he needs. We press, pull, thrust against each other like two teenagers doing it in the backseat of their parents' car for the first time. Neither one of us take a moment to temper our moans and shouts, we don't care about who can hear us, and as I feel him spill into the condom between us, it sends me over the edge.

The only thing I wish was different? That we hadn't had the condom at all, because I have a feeling sex with nothing between us? It's going to be even more mind-blowing than this was.

CHAPTER NINETEEN

Cutter

"I HAVE TO GO," I remind her, whispering softly.

The breath I exhale disturbs the hair at her temple. The sun has risen into the sky, shining brightly through her window. We saw every hour last night, including the moon.

"I wish you didn't." She holds onto my waist tightly.

Her small voice kills me. It would hurt less if you filleted my chest open, exposing my heart. "I don't want to, but I need to get back to Laurel Springs."

Although I'm not sure what my life is going to be like there now. Thinking about the place I've loved since I was a kid doesn't make me excited anymore. When I close my eyes it's hard to imagine the streets in vivid colors and the people I love, like I've always been able to do. That color is now slightly muted, the voices of my family not as loud as they once were.

"I know." She pulls herself from me, sitting cross-legged in the bed, not bothering to cover her form. The long hair

I've wanted to see down flows over her chest, only separating where her upturned breasts force her nipples to peek through.

Reaching up, I flex my hand around her neck, pulling her mouth down to mine. It's a chaste kiss, still full of possession, but acknowledging we don't have the time either one of us wants. Bringing my forehead against hers, I close my eyes, inhaling her scent, hoping to imprint it on my skin. "Didn't expect you," I press the words out from between my lips. "Thought I was gonna come down here, do a job, and head back home."

She giggles, but I can feel the wetness of a tear sliding between our cheeks. "When they told me the LSERT was coming, I was like shit, here we go. These people are gonna come here and try to tell us how to do our jobs. They're gonna feel sorry for us and make us feel less than what we are. I didn't expect you either."

Forcing my hand between us, I use my thumb to swipe away the moisture from her face. "Please don't cry for me," I choke out. "Please. We'll see each other again."

"Will we? Will we make this work?"

"I want it to," I say, the promise there in my voice. The most important promise I've ever made.

"Me too," she answers. "But more than anything I don't want to let you walk out of the door today."

"I don't either, but I've got to take Tucker's truck back to him, I have to report to work next week."

"I get it." She pulls her hair back, exposing herself to me. "We both have lives, mine will get back to normal quicker than I anticipate and yours has been going out without you."

Those words are the truest anyone has ever said to me and it's something I don't think I realized. Life has been going on without me at home. While I've been down south trying to figure out how to help, my family has been going on as status quo. What is everyone going to be like when I get home? It's been almost two weeks, not like I've been gone for years, but the things I've seen here will stay with me forever. The hurricane, the aftermath, and meeting Rowan. This has all changed the trajectory of how I thought my life would progress.

"I wonder how much my nephew's grown."

Even though I saw him when I FaceTimed with Stella, it's not seeing him in person. He always looks much bigger in person.

"Probably more than you ever thought he could."

She's got this far-off look in her eyes. One she gets a lot when we discuss Keegan. Even though I want to ask her about it, I don't want to ruin what little time we have left this morning.

"You gonna text me?" I change the subject.

She smiles. "Only if you text me. Can't expect me to make the first move. I'm not a loose woman." She turns her torso away from me, bashfully hiding her face.

"Oh yeah?" I reach up, palming the underside of her breast. "Yet here you are, sitting here without a shirt one, showing me all your goods. You do that to everybody?" I tease.

"You know you're the only one who's seen my goods in a long time."

It's the last thing we have time for, but I have to leave here with her taste on my tongue. I need to immerse myself in her before I go. Pressing on her stomach, I push her back to the bed, nudging my way in between her thighs.

"We don't have time, Cutter."

Scooting down so that I'm on my stomach, my shoulders spreading her apart. "We always have time for this."

I dive in, hoping to sate myself on the taste of her. I know I won't be able to, but I can at least survive until we see each other again. At least that's what I tell myself as I push my arms under her thighs, hook them over her hips, and spread her lips apart. Leaning in, I blow a breath to let her know I'm here, which causes her to reach down, threading her fingers through my hair, yanking on it roughly. Lifting my eyes, they meet hers as she watches me.

I keep them open until I can't see her anymore, closing them before I reach in with my tongue and lave the bud begging for my attention.

Her thighs tighten against me, but I hold her open, proving I'm either the stronger or the more stubborn of the two of us.

"Cutter..."

That breathless voice, that's what I needed to hear one more time before I leave, before I fucking say goodbye to the piece of heaven I've found in the middle of destruction rained down like hell.

Just my luck, huh? I find the one thing I can't live without during the most unpredictable time in my life. That's how it's always been, and I presume it's how it'll always be. At least it's taught to me to appreciate things while we have them.

And right now, I have Rowan at my fingertips, or rather at the tip of my tongue. Suctioning my mouth over the part of her that needs me the most, I suck, lick, and do everything I can think of to turn her into a quivering mass of jelly within my arms.

"God, I didn't know you could do that," she groans as I

clasp her clit between my teeth while circling it with my tongue. "I didn't know half of what you do to me could be done."

There's a pride in my chest, it makes me want to thump and proclaim her mine. But do I really have a claim on her when I have to leave? It feels unfair and maybe slightly premature to just assume, but I can't help it. I want her. Maybe it's selfish, but for once in my life I deserve to be selfish.

My cellphone rings, and I know it's Tucker, calling to check and see where I am. I refuse to answer it, refuse to stop what I'm doing right now, because I can't stand to not finish this.

Pulling back, I unhook one of my arms, using two fingers to go after her hard. I need to hear her release, I need the taste it on my tongue, ache to have her smell all over me until I wash it off.

"Come for me," I pant, flexing my forearm.

"Cutter," she whines, pressing her hips up into my thrust.

Her clit enlarges, causing me to lean forward and take it between my lips again, using my tongue to go after it like she did my dick.

The phone rings again, but I don't stop, can't stop. Her thighs are tightening around me, and I know she's close, but she just can't get there. Grabbing her around the hips, I flip over so that she's on my face.

For a split second, I take my hands off her body, reach up, grab her hands, and put them on the headboard. Then I'm back to her hips, showing her how to ride my tongue.

In this position she seems to lose it, moans fall out of her mouth as she rotates her mound against my mouth, grinding down hard. I don't stop as I continue to lick at her swollen flesh.

Then out of nowhere, she reaches behind her, grabbing my cock in her hand. It's engorged, hard, and ready to explode. She strokes me up and down as I stroke her. The two of us are pushing each other headlong into an explosion of both our bodies.

Part of me wants to hold out because I don't know when I'll see her again, don't know what our future holds. I wish I could take a picture of us right now, to have later when I want to relive the absolute sexiness of this moment. If there's anything that'll get me through leaving her, it'll be knowing I have this memory.

She stops stroking me, plunging her fingers into my hair, she holds me tightly to her body. Straightening my tongue, I let her ride it as I reach down, grabbing my own cock in my hands. Together we come in a mess of grunts, screams, and thundering hearts.

As she gets off me, I lick my lips, thankful I'll leave with the taste of her on them.

CHAPTER TWENTY

Rowan

TEARS STREAM down my face as I watch them leave.

There's no one here to hug me, no one to assure me it's going to all work out the way it's supposed to. I could have asked Sullivan to come, but then I'd have to explain to him about Cutter, and for now I want to keep all our memories to myself. I'm not a big fan of leaving things up to chance, but this is one of those times I'll have to have some trust. I don't have a crystal ball and I don't know what the future will bring.

Not even sure I wanna know what the future has in store for me. It's burnt me more than once. In bigger ways than I ever thought it could.

My eyes follow the taillights of the vehicles until they're gone. They're a blip on the horizon and I know I need to leave. It'll do me no good to stand here and wish things were different.

Feeling completely hollow, I walk over to my car and get

in, starting the engine. It's still warm here in the south, so I crank up my air conditioner, turn on the radio and take a drive I know very well. It's so ingrained in me, I can do it with my eyes closed.

It's been about a month since I was here last, and I'm almost ashamed of myself. There was a time when I would come here every single day, sometimes twice a day. Back then I never thought I'd go a month, and yet here I am.

Turning into the tree-lined drive, I'm pleased to see they've taken care of any damage they may have sustained. Again, I'm disappointed with myself, I should have been here before now. It's a maze of headstones, but I know exactly where the one I want to see is located. When I get to it, I pull over to the side and park.

Instead of the overwhelming sadness I used to have when I came here, today it's making me feel not so alone. She's here, even if she's not. I almost run up the rows, to the edge of where her grave is. Getting there, I take a seat on the grass, the way I've always done.

"Hey, Etta," I whisper, glancing at the picture on the gravestone. She'll be forever memorialized as a four-year-old.

Reaching up, I trace her smile, the length of her hair, and the small cleft she had in her chin. She had the best giggle, always finding the humor in every situation. When I'd go wake her up, she'd wake up stretching and smiling. I'd reach down, tickling her stomach slightly, and she'd start her little-girl giggle. This is my favorite memory of her, not the memory of pulling her out of the water while her dad stood to the side, frozen with what he said was fear, and I said was cowardice.

"I miss you," I tell her. "We had a hurricane, but we did okay making it through. Your Uncle Sully has been taking care of so many. I haven't been by to see Grandma and Grandpa, but I will," I promise her. They were two of her favorite people, and I know she wants to hear how they're doing.

"I met this guy." I pull at the blades of grass. "I think you'd like him."

She and her dad were never close, it was the one thing she'd needed in her life, but I did my best to make her feel love, regardless of how much he did or didn't show it.

"He'd probably go to the playground with you and push you on the swings until his arms were exhausted. We could've all gone to the lake on Grandpa's boat. He'd ride with you on the inner tube. There were so many things I wanted to do with you, Etta. So much I wanted you to experience, so much I wanted to watch you experience." I feel tears sliding down my face.

"And it kills me," I choke out. "Because I don't feel at home here anymore."

I said it, the words I've been feeling for close to a year. Paradise Lost hasn't felt like home. "But you're here," I continue, wiping at the tears. "I'm not sure if I can let you go."

"You don't have to be here to be close to her."

My mother's voice scares me to death, I jump as I turn around to look at her.

"I'm sorry." She sinks down on the grass next to me. "I said your name a few times, but you didn't hear me. I hadn't been out here since Tatum, and I wanted to make sure everything was still okay."

"Me too." I lean into her shoulder as she put her arm around my neck.

"Where have you been lately? We've seen Sully and

Braylon, but not you. That's unusual Ro, we're worried about you."

"I don't even know where to start," I whisper to my mom. "You know the Laurel Springs Emergency Response Team came to help us in the wake of Tatum, right?"

"Yeah, your daddy told me all about it. Sullivan even road with an EMT for a few days, if I remember correctly."

"Right, the EMT Sullivan rode with, he and I became friendly."

My cheeks heat as I try to convey to her what friendly means while not exactly telling her we screwed each other's brains out. That not three hours ago, I was spread out on my bed with his head between my legs.

"You don't have to be embarrassed, honey, you had a baby at eighteen. We know you've had sex."

I pull my knees up to my chin.

"What makes this guy different?"

I've wondered this myself, but I haven't been able to put my finger on it. Why is Cutter so much different than any of the other guys I dated? Why has he been able to get under my skin without even seeming to have to try? "He listened to me." I look over at her, resting my cheek on my knees. "And he doesn't know about Etta."

Her eyes scrutinize me, squinting as she looks over my face. "Do you think that's wise, Rowan? Etta's a huge part of your past."

"That's just it," I push out, frustrated. "She's my past, and everybody always judges me by my past. Everybody knows what happened with her, and with Tommie." My coward of an ex-husband. "In this town, I can't get over it. People look at me with that sadness in their eyes - because they know - everyone knows my daughter drowned. They know I had a nervous breakdown after I couldn't save her, and they know I blame Tommie."

"It was an accident, Rowan," Mom tries, like she was always does.

"He was supposed to be watching her." I ball my hand up into a fist. "It was the only job he had that day, he didn't have to work, I was the one coming home from a fourteen-hour shift. All he had to do was watch her." My voice breaks as I try to get my breath. "He went inside for a beer, Mom. For a fucking beer, then he got distracted. He didn't even know she'd gone into the water." Tears are now streaming down my face.

"Do you know she probably screamed for help?" I ask her. "She probably screamed for help, wondered where her mom and dad were. We were so proud of that damn house with the stupid pool." I grab at the blades of grass, yanking them out with more ferociousness than I should.

"You should have been proud." She puts her hand over mine. "Y'all worked hard to get that house. The two of you were so young, nobody thought you'd make it."

I cut her off. "And we didn't, did we? The thought of her screaming for help keeps me up at night, Mama, and I can't for the life of me find it in my heart to forgive Tommie. He stood by and watched me," I tell her, for the first time. "When I came in the door, asking where Etta was, and he told me outside. I knew, call it mother's intuition, call it whatever you want. I knew she was in trouble. As soon as I walked out the back door I could see her hair, she was floating face down. I screamed at him to grab her and he didn't. He stood there, beer in his hand."

"Rowan, we all deal with emergencies differently." She holds my hand in hers.

"He's an EMT, just like me." I shake my head. "He knew what to do. He knew what to do and he let her die. He didn't even try to help me with CPR. You can tell me we all deal with emergencies differently until you're blue in the face, but I'll never forgive him." I shake my head.

"Her eyes were open, and I'll never be able to get that out of my head, just like I'll never be able to look at him again without seeing the man who let my daughter die. It might be wrong, but God can judge me for it when it's my time."

Mom doesn't say anything else, instead she sits with me in silence as we look at Etta's grave. She was my life, she was everything I lived for. Now I need to decide if I'm going to live for myself.

Nobody else is going to do it for me.

CHAPTER TWENTY-ONE

Cutter

ONE WEEK **Later**

"Your mom misses you."

A heavy sigh releases from my chest. "You sure it's my mom?"

Turning around, I see Dad standing behind me. I'm using the LSPD's workout room to train today, but I honestly didn't expect to run into him.

"We all miss you," Holden Thompson says as he stands in front of me. My dad has always been one of my favorite people, but since I've come back from Paradise Lost, things just haven't felt right. I've been doing my best, but my heart isn't in what's going on here.

"I know." I grab hold of my t-shirt, pulling it over my head. Pulling it down, I stride to the treadmill and get on. Dad does the same thing.

"What are you doing?"

He gives me a look. "Spending some time with my son.

Ransom told me you aren't talking to him either, and I have a feeling you need to talk to someone."

I hate when he's right, really bugs the shit out of me. Even though he's my favorite person, he can still get on my nerves.

"What makes you think I need to talk to someone?" I start off at a slow pace, working to increase my speed.

"You're way too much like me. Everybody says Ransom is, but you are. When you're bothered, you close off and shut down. Which is exactly what you've been doing since you came back. Why don't you tell me what happened?"

"Because" - I can feel my redden in agitation and embarrassment - "I don't like talking about shit, especially after what happened in Tuscaloosa."

"Years ago, Cutter," he reminds me. "What happened there happened years ago. You've grown up, you've changed. Trust me enough to tell me what's going on with you."

I don't know why I'm fighting this so much. Back in the day, I would've told him anything, except he didn't ask. Ransom had been the one I'd confided in and I'd almost begged Dad to ask me. Now he's finally doing what I've wanted him to do, and I'm fighting against it.

"I met a girl."

The easiest way I know how to explain, but it doesn't encompass my feelings at all.

"It's always about a girl." He grins.

"I wish it was that easy." I grin back over to him. "This feels like I'm losing my mind."

"That's love, Cutter. Open up and let me help you."

My feet are pounding out a welcome rhythm, one I haven't heard in much too long. It isn't that I don't want to let my dad help me, it's that I don't want to make myself vulnerable again. No one knew how to deal with me after I came back from Tuscaloosa, and I'm not sure if this will put me in the same headspace. On the other side of the coin, I would love to hear what my dad has to say. He and mom have been successfully married for a lot of years, and he knows how to make a marriage last.

"Her name is Rowan and she's an EMT down in Paradise Lost."

He makes a noise in his throat. "So you met under highly stressful circumstances, which means the attraction was probably tenfold because of your adrenaline."

"You could say that."

"So why are you here and she's there?"

Shaking my head, I have to chuckle at the old man. "Maybe because she's got a life there and I've got a life here. Neither one of us can really pack up and leave."

"Invite her here, I'd love to meet her."

"Oh my God, I just bet you would. Why do I get the feeling I'm going to be the talk of next family dinner?"

"I mean nobody else has anything going on in their lives." He shrugs, not even slightly ashamed. "Not to mention, we've been waiting on you to move on from Tuscaloosa for a long time."

Move on.

Have I?

Teenage Cutter had hurt, hurt in ways he hadn't been able to forget for years. It had hung around at the back of his mind every time he'd met a new girl. Each date he'd try to take one of them out on, he'd wondered why were they really there for him? Was it because they liked him, or because someone else had put them up to it? Was I still teenage Cutter?

"Truth is, I don't know if I'm over it."

"Then you need to tell her about it." Dad reaches over, grabbing the bottle of water I have propped on my treadmill. He opens it, taking a drink, while I look on with my mouth open in astonishment. "You need to let her know your fears, that way you can't push her. We all need love, Cut. You, more than others, because you're such a sensitive soul. It's time to let it in."

Can I do that though?

"Maybe I'm not meant to be like you and Ransom. Find the love of your lives and settle down forever. Have the house and the kid. Maybe that's not me. By the way, that's my damn water."

He stops his treadmill, giving me a look of disbelief. "You and I both know that's a load of horse shit. If anyone in this family is meant to be married, it's you. I don't know why you're trying to act like you're too good for it. I'm older, I need to stay hydrated."

God, I hate when he's right.

"So what do you think I should do."

I swear, his eyes light up like I've just given him the best Christmas present in the history of Christmas presents. If there's one thing Holden Thompson likes to do, it's telling others how they should be living their lives. Guess Ransom hasn't been seeking him out for advice lately.

"Invite her here. See if the two of you mesh during your everyday lives, not just when you're stuck in a situation where you're constantly having to be on. It's the everyday shit that counts. Like me going to help your mom at The Café, taking care of Keegan so Ransom and Stella can spend some time together. That's the stuff that counts in the long run. That stuff? It makes marriages."

"I should just invite her? Be like 'Hey, why don't you come up to Laurel Springs and get interrogated by my family. It'll be a great time for all involved'."

"You say it like it's a bad thing, Cutter. We love you."

"Y'all are nosey."

"Every family is, just deal with it. You know we were nosey about Stella, too."

"That's bullshit," I argue. "You knew her, her whole life. There was nothing to be nosey about."

"Nothing to be nosey about? They didn't tell anyone they were dating for months, Cutter. Or did you forget?"

I roll my eyes. "How could I?"

"Look, smartass, I don't love your attitude, but I understand it. Invite her up here and I promise we won't embarrass you. Just let us get to know her, let her get to know us. You haven't given us that option - ever."

What he's said has its merits and he's right, I've never let a woman in my life come here, never introduced her to my family. Not after college, and if I'm serious about Rowan, I should be willing to try new things with her.

"Okay," I answer finally.

"Okay?"

"I'll ask her if she wants to come here, but this will be on her terms. I'm not forcing her to do anything she doesn't want to do."

Dad looks so proud of himself, so pleased that he was able to wear me down. Pisses me off so bad.

"That's fair." He reaches out, bumping my knuckles with his.

"More than fair, and let me just say. When she comes here," - because I refuse to believe she won't; I need to see her as much as I need air to breathe - "you aren't allowed to monopolize her time."

"Got it, no monopolizing." He holds up his hands in mock-surrender.

"I mean it, Dad. Tell Mom, too."

He crosses his heart. "I promise, we'll be on our best behavior."

Something tells me he's lying through his teeth, but I'll take what I can get at this point. He's off the treadmill, grabbing a towel and heading out the door.

"Don't you have the rest of your workout to finish?"

"Already done." He grins, waving goodbye.

Ugh... I've been played.

Going over to my stuff, I grab my cellphone out of my bag, pulling up Rowan's contact information. We've texted a few times here and there, both trying to figure out how we fit into each other's lives now.

Closing my eyes I send up a little prayer that she'll say yes. I'm not sure how I'll handle it if she doesn't.

Heart. Broken.

A little piece of my brain says. It's loud enough so that I can hear it.

"Shut the fuck up," I mumble. "It's now or never."

C: How would you feel about coming up to spend the weekend with me? I'm off and I'd love to see you. I miss you.

I wonder if I should have put the I miss you on there, but I realize I need to be myself. Not being honest is what screwed up the last true relationship I was in. I'll be as honest as I can, no matter how much it exposes me to potential hurt.

R: Ya know what? I'd love to. It'll do me good to get out of town for a few days. Are you sure you're okay with it?

A smile spreads across my face.

C: I'm ecstatic about it. Let's make plans!

CHAPTER TWENTY-TWO

Rowan

I'VE NEVER BEEN SO excited to take a road trip. In fact, I can't remember the last one I took. Maybe when I was sixteen and some friends and I went to a concert in Birmingham. After I got pregnant with Etta things changed, and then after she died, I changed.

As I hit I-65 North, my heart feels less heavy, and the more I leave Paradise Lost in the background, a smile spreads across my face easier than it has in years.

Reaching over, I turn up the radio, open my sunroof, and put the car on cruise control. The GPS says I have an hour and a half to go with most of my travel being on this section of interstate.

Glancing at my rearview, I get a picture of myself in the reflection I wasn't expecting. One I haven't seen in years. My hair is down, blowing in the breeze, my eyes are full of life and my skin is pink with excitement. I almost don't know myself, but at the same time I do know her. She's the me I've always wanted to be.

When I stop at a rest area, I dial Cutter's number as I walk to the bathrooms.

"Hey," he answers. His deep voice always brings a smile to my face and chills up and down my body. Talking with him on the phone is so intimate, and I'm lucky I get to be the one to do it.

"Hey yourself. I just wanted to let you know I'm about forty-five minutes out, I'm stopping at a rest area.

There's a lot of noise behind him, I can hear a small kid playing in the background.

"You're so close." I can hear the smile in his voice. "Keegan, leave Rambo alone. He's tired."

"Are you babysitting?"

He sighs. "Something like that. Look, I hate to do this to you, but my family has pounced, they want to meet you. They're having a cookout tonight at my brother and sister-in-law's house."

I can tell he's trying to gauge how I feel by the slow way he speaks the words.

"If you don't want to do this, say the word and I'll leave. I'm slightly pissed they did this, but they love me and they want to get to know you."

There's a nervousness in my stomach I haven't had in a long time, but I almost welcome it.

"It's fine, I'm excited to meet your family." I realize how honest those words are I wonder who I've become. I've never wanted to meet people, but again the farther I've gotten away from Paradise Lost, the more the tightness in my chest has relaxed. The more colorful things seem to have gotten, the color of the sky and the brightness of the green grass is something I haven't noticed - in I don't know how long.

"Okay, so let me give you the address to my brother's house. That's where we all are. There will be dogs and children here. Are you okay with that?"

"Yes, Cutter." I grin. "Nothing is going to keep me away from you today."

"I'm so glad to hear it."

"Can you text me the info, I really have to use the restroom. It's why I stopped."

"Yeah, see you soon."

I hang up, excited at this prospect of meeting new people. They don't know my backstory; they can't look at me with sadness and pity in their eyes. There will be no whispers.

Is she the girl who lost her daughter? The one who died in their back yard because of the swimming pool? She's so young. Bless her heart.

For once, I just want to be the new girl in town, maybe a little secretive and aloof, but I want my own backstory. I want to share it when I want, and refuse when I don't.

As I open the door to the restrooms, I square my shoulders and decide whatever happens today will be because I want it to, and not because I'm reacting to how others are treating me. They'll meet the old Rowan, the one who wasn't scared of anything, who enjoyed socializing and being someone others could talk to. I'm going to pull her out and dust her off, give her permission to shine. She may be tarnished, but that's nothing a little cleaner won't fix.

WHEN I SEE the signs indicating Laurel Springs is the next exit, I excitedly beat my palms against the steering wheel. I'm that much closer to seeing Cutter. Texts and a few FaceTime's over the week haven't been enough. It's crazy how he became such an important part of my life in a short amount of time. I guess that could be said for a lot of things, though but this one, this one I'm really happy about.

Following the directions given to me, I pull into a really nice residential neighborhood. It's the type of place I would love to build a family in, which catches me off-guard because I haven't thought about having a family since I lost the one I had.

Glancing down, I see the house is close, and that's when I see all the cars and trucks parked in the driveway. I find a place for my car to fit, then reach over, texting Cutter that I'm here.

Nervously I sit in my car, waiting for him to appear, and when he does, I can't help but get out and running to him. You'd think we haven't seen each other in months, instead of days. He catches me as I get to him, palming my thighs as I wrap them around his waist, pulling my mouth to his. This kiss shouldn't be made public, but it is what it is. We've obviously missed each other a ton.

When he pulls back, she smiles widely. "Your hair."

"What about it?"

"It's down, and you only wear it down when you trust somebody."

He repeats the words I've told him back at me. He says it with a wonderment, and it makes my heart beat just a little faster. This man has listened to me, he's taken what I've said into his soul, and he's given it back to me.

"I trust you," I whisper, kissing him again. "Otherwise I wouldn't be here right now."

He groans. "I'm so sorry this got sprung on you. If you're not having a good time, we'll leave."

"No, I think I'll like this."

He puts me down, hugging me tightly. "Just remember that offer stands for any time of the night."

"Got it."

He grabs my hand, pulling me into what I assume is a back yard. A dog barks, a toddler screeches as he runs away from the dog with a ball in hand.

"Keegan and Rambo. They're playing fetch, but Keegan hasn't figured out he's supposed to throw the ball for Rambo to go and get yet."

I giggle as I watch them. A sprinkler is set up, and as they run through it, Keegan giggles, Rambo barks in appreciation.

"Keegan looks a lot like you."

"The Thompson genes are very dominant." He winks at me.

Pulling me over to what I assume is his family, he starts off. "Y'all, this is Rowan, be nice to her, don't tell her about my bad habits, and for fuck's sake, don't question her about every single thing dealing with how we got together."

I gasp, shocked he would say this to his family, but they seem to take it in stride.

"Rowan, going around the circle here. My dad Holden, mom Leigh, brother Ransom, sister-in-law Stella, cute kid is Keegan, goodest of all boys is Rambo. Fam, this is Rowan."

"Nice to meet you." I wave to them, slightly embarrassed.

"I'll do my best to not say anything about you wearing an Auburn t-shirt into my house," the one he introduced as

Stella says. I recognize her from when she called after Cutter sent her the selfie we took. "But my mom's coming over later, and I can't make promises for her. Just know she's serious about her football and she'll see your shirt as shots fired."

I shrug. "I can take it, I'm used to it. I'm one of the only girls on the EMT squad and everyone else is a 'Bama fan. She can't say anything worse than what I've heard before."

They all look at each other, and I wonder what the hell I've gotten myself into.

"Are you hungry?" Leigh asks, clapping her hands. "Food is almost ready, we were waiting on you to do the last few things."

My stomach growls so loud I'm surprised they can't hear it. "Starving! Is there anything I can do to help?"

"Your job is to sit here and talk to me." Cutter pulls me down beside him on a bench. "We watch the dog and the kid while we catch up on what's happened with our lives the last few days."

"Sounds good to me."

And as I look out at the yard, watching everybody get up to go do their parts and see the curly head of the kid running back and forth with the dog, I realize this doesn't hurt. It would've any other time, but not here with Cutter, with his family, and in this town.

It doesn't hurt.

I want more of this, and I want to keep it for as long as I can.

Truthfully I don't know what that means, but I'm willing to explore it. All I know, is I'm not sure my place is in Paradise Lost anymore, but I'm not sure it's here either.

There's only one way to find out.

CHAPTER TWENTY-THREE

Cutter

SO FAR EVERYONE'S been on their best behavior, but when I see Whitney and Ryan making their way through the back door, I immediately grasp Rowan's hand.

"Awww shit."

"What?" she asks as she looks to where my gaze is pinned.

"Look, whatever Whitney says about you wearing an Auburn shirt, just let it go one ear and out the other."

This time Rowan gives me a serious look. "How do you expect me to do that? We're rivals."

"Because you're here with me and I want us to have a nice night?"

My voice is hopeful, even I can hear it.

"College football is serious, Cutter. You should know that."

Oh how I do, and how I know Whitney will never let this go.

"Cutter, is this the lady I've heard so much about?"

She's already spotted us and is coming over with Keegan in her arms. He's a spoiled boy by both sets of grandparents and he revels in the attention.

"It sure is. Whitney, this is Rowan, Rowan, this is Whitney."

Their eyes zero in on what each other is wearing.

"Fuck," I breathe.

"Fuck!" Keegan parrots.

"Cutter..."

Everyone in the back yard looks at me. I simply flip them off, watching in horror as Keegan does the same.

Ransom comes over to get his son. "You know he does every single thing you do. That was irresponsible."

So now I'm leading my nephew down a path of irresponsibility and self-righteousness. Good to know. "Sorry," I manage to whisper, before I rub the back of my neck.

Before I can even say anything to Whitney, she's opened her mouth, and I notice she's rubbing her pearls. She's probably asking God for my forgiveness in her head.

"I hope you enjoy that one little victory y'all got at the Iron Bowl," she indicates Rowan's shirt. "We're taking it back this year."

There's a part of me that hopes Rowan won't rise to the bait, but I know how serious this rivalry is.

"Oh how the mighty have fallen."

"That's right." Whitney grins. "Our eight, or was it nine-year winning streak was too heavy a burden for us to hold. We got bored proving how bad your team was."

There's a round of oohhh's in the backyard.

I want to cover my head and come back up for air once this is all over.

"Ryan, help me," I beg.

"Oh no, I don't get between my wife and the Tide. You should know that by now."

"Whitney, please be nice, I want her to stay."

"I ain't gonna run her off, Cutter. I'll just bless her heart and give her an Alabama shirt at Christmas."

I look at Rowan, scared to death about what she might be thinking. Please don't let her be ready to leave. I should have warned her about Whitney, but I hadn't known she was going to show up. To my relief, Rowan giggles. She giggles so hard she has tears streaming down her face.

"I like you," she gasps while holding her stomach. "It'll be so much fun to watch the Iron Bowl with you."

"You just wait." Whitney grins. "Stella and I have a lucky bullet. We'll tell you all about that story."

My eyes widen as I glance at my sister-in-law. "Y'all have a lucky bullet? What the fuck is wrong with y'all?"

"Don't judge, Cutter. You might not like what you'd get judged for." Stella sticks her tongue out at me.

"I just don't even ask anymore," Ransom says as he comes to stand beside me. "I mean, do not get between these two and their football. It's the only way Ryan and I have stayed alive, married to them."

"Let's eat," Mom says, clapping her hands, and I've never been more excited to sit down at a table and go through an inquisition before in my life.

"THIS IS REALLY GOOD," Rowan tells me as she takes a bite of her potato salad. "Your mom is a great cook."

"She owns a restaurant." I nod over to her. "The Café, it's the most popular in town."

"I wouldn't say that," Mom says, putting her fork down. "We've cut our hours back because I'm just too old to keep working there all the time."

"You should retire," all three men in her life say at the same time.

"If you can't tell, they all have an opinion about how I should live my life." She grins over at Rowan.

Rowan giggles. "They seem to have very solid opinions."

"I let them think they have a say so." She winks.

At the other end of the table, Keegan starts screaming.

"What did you do?" I ask Ransom, who sits there with a blank look on his face, staring at his son.

"Wiped ketchup off his forehead. Apparently I've gravely injured him."

Rambo whines, wanting to get up to where Keegan is, so he can make sure his buddy isn't hurt. The two of them have such a great relationship.

"Let me take him inside." Stella gets up from where she sits a few seats down. "He didn't have a nap and he's probably tired. Either we or I will be back in a few."

Giving my brother a smartass grin, I needle him. "Wanna have more, huh? What about that baseball team you were gonna have?"

"Shut the fuck up." He throws a roll at me. "We've reevaluated the baseball team."

Everyone laughs at him. "You always learn how many you can handle," Mom says as she looks between the two of us. Like when I had Cutter, along with Ransom, I realized there would be no way I could handle any more. You two were more than enough."

Ryan nods over to my dad. "I can remember Havoc saying that a time or two when we'd ask where the girl was. He always wanted to try for a girl."

"Cutter ruined it." Ransom lifts his glass up in salute.

"Ransom ruined it." I raise my glass up to him. "Once I came along and he wasn't the favorite anymore, he bitched like a pansy."

"I promise," - Mom looks at Rowan - "they love each other. They wouldn't take anything for their brother, but when they get together, they act like this."

"Me and my brothers are the exact same way." She grins. "Actually, they're worse, because they're guys and they're cops."

"Cops?" Dad asks. "What's your last name again?"

"Baker."

"Your dad the chief of police down there? I've met him a few times, he's a really good guy."

"Yeah." She nods, taking a drink of her water. "He's going to retire this year, though."

"Is that right? Is Sullivan going to take his spot?"

"That's the plan, but Braylon would like it too. I'm not sure how they're going to go about giving it away, but the two of them will fight to the death for it. Braylon's on desk duty right now though."

Dad makes a noise. "I heard about that. Got shot in the knee?"

"He did, I was actually the responding EMT. One of the scariest nights of my life."

"I can imagine."

My mind wanders, it's one of the scariest things for me to. Each time I hear we're going to a call where a member of Laurel Springs PD might be injured, I think about all the men I know on the force. In my mind I try to decide where they all might be and pray that they aren't in the line of danger. Really though, each time they go out, they are, and there's nothing any of us can do about it. Ransom's been shot once and thank God I wasn't an EMT then. I'm not sure I'll ever be able to get the sight of my brother on my stretcher out of my mind.

"You okay?" Rowan asks, bumping my elbow. "You got really quiet."

"Just trying to figure out how you dealt with a family member being on your stretcher."

The smile that was on her face disappears and I want to kick myself for it. If we were in a much more private setting I ask what was going through that head of hers. "You just have to compartmentalize it. Having family members in the line of duty doesn't change the oath you take. More than anything you're probably going to work harder to save them."

I know she's said the truth, but I worry I'll freeze. What if I let my brother down? The one who's never let me down before?

"Hey, don't think about it," Rowan whispers in my ear. "The more you think about it, the more you get in your head about it. Your training will take over and you won't even know what you've done."

"Is that what happened with you?"

I can tell she doesn't want to answer the question, but she does and for that I'm grateful.

"Yeah, everything I did was by the book, because I'd been trained that way. I was on autopilot and didn't even have a chance to question myself. Don't overthink it. The minute you overthink it, it allows for doubts to seep in. We know our training, and our training is what gets us through the hard times and rough days."

I put my arm around her neck, pulling her close as I drop as kiss on her forehead. On the one hand, I hope she's right, on the other I hope I'm never in the position where I have to test myself.

But that's a prayer for another day.

CHAPTER TWENTY-FOUR

Rowan

"I'M SO sorry you had to be thrown before the firing squad."

I'm not exactly sure what he's talking about. "The firing squad?"

"Yeah, my nosey as fuck family."

"They're nice." And they really are. No one has made me feel more welcome. "Your mom said there's family breakfast at The Café tomorrow?"

"We don't have to go if you don't want to. I promise no one will say anything."

"It's okay, we can go. I liked them a lot. I like how they love you." I kneel on the bed, walking on my knees over to him.

"They're suffocating."

I push my arms around his neck, holding him tightly. "You're their favorite person, I think. You're at least Keegan's favorite person and Ransom loves you like crazy."

His eyes soften. "I love them a lot too. Ya know my dad and I had a conversation about love the other day."

"Oh really?"

My pulse gets faster, I'm not sure what he's going to say to me.

"Yeah, I told him you scare the fuck out of me."

"I scare you?"

"So much."

I scrutinize his face, enjoying the little freckles that have popped up on his nose, the way his beard is starting to grow in this late at night. "How do I scare you?"

"Before I met you, I couldn't see the rest of my life. I had no idea what I was going to do with it. To be honest, I kinda thought I'd ride along and never make any kind of commitment to anyone."

"Why did you think that?"

He swallows roughly. "Because of what happened to me in college."

His family alluded to this, and he's made several cryptic statements. More than anything I want to know what happened, but I know we both have secrets, and if he shares this one, I'll need to share mine. Can I do that?

For the first time I think I can. If I trust anyone with how I felt, it's him.

Which is odd because I've always thought you can't know anyone and their heart in a couple of weeks. How I feel about Cutter proves my assumption is so very, very wrong.

"Can you trust me with what happened?"

He nods, but doesn't say anything.

"If I'm gonna talk about this, I'm gonna need a beer. You wanna go to the commons area?"

"The commons area?"

A perk of this apartment building is we have a fire pit with seating out back. Anyone can use it, and at this time of night, no one will be there.

"If it'll help you." I hug him tightly. "Whatever will help you."

"It will." He grabs hold of my hand, helping me off the bed.

As we leave his apartment, he takes a detour to his kitchen to grab a bottle of beer. "You want one?"

I nod, who knows what he's going to say. Maybe this will completely change the way our relationship has been going up to this point. I'm equal parts nervous and thankful he trusts me enough to tell me the truth.

We're quite as we take the elevator down to the lobby. He holds my hand tightly, like he's afraid I'm going to bolt as soon as he lets it go. I want badly to tell him I'll never bolt, but the truth is I'm not sure. I've reacted in so many different ways over the past few years, I don't even recognize myself anymore.

The one thing I do know? I want to be here for him in any way he needs me to be. When we get outside, I can tell why he wanted to come here. It's a little piece of serenity in the middle of this town. Comfortable seating, a fire pit, and more privacy than we probably have in his apartment.

"I don't even know where to begin," he starts, taking a drink of his beer. "There are so many things that mush together in this story."

"Why don't you start at the beginning?"

"For so long I wasn't sure where the beginning was." He looks over, a sad smile on his face. "But I've been thinking about this a lot, knowing I wanted to tell you about it, and I think I realize it started my senior year of high school. I was aggressively recruited."

"For football?"

I don't want to assume and I want to get the entire gist of what he's telling me.

"Yeah, for football. Auburn, Alabama, Florida State, UT, they all wanted me. But I had a kinship with Alabama because my friend Caleb went there, and he loved it."

"Also, your family." I quirk my brow, thinking of Whitney and Stella.

"Oh yeah, they would have disowned me for sure. Even though they weren't married yet."

"I'd toured all the campuses and I wasn't really sure where I wanted to go, each one had something different to offer. In the end I was stuck between Florida State and Alabama. I toured FSU and was ninety percent sure I was going to sign with them, but Dad suggested I tour Alabama one more time."

"Always a good idea." I take a drink of my beer, already a bad feeling building in my stomach.

"We went down there and they had me a damn parade. Which was just weird to be honest. I was an eighteen-year-old kid. What did I do for a parade? If anyone should have had a parade, it was my dad and uncles. But my fragile ego..." He shakes his head, taking another drink. "I thought I deserved it."

"I mean, football in the south..."

"Yeah, football in the south. So that day there were a few people who helped me around campus. One of them was a girl named Katie. Actually it was Katherine, but she went by Katie. She had her red lipstick, blonde hair, and pearls around her neck. She wore her southern debutante costume with a pride I have yet to see again."

"Oh no," I whisper.

"We hit it off. She was everything I wanted in a girl. From the moment I met her, she flirted with me, and I was flattered. She was a junior, older than me, and the things she said, the things she did - sexually - were things I'd only heard of." His face gets red. I'm unsure if it's from anger or embarrassment.

"We dated for almost two years. I told her I loved her, first girl I ever said that word too, and I was making a plan to declare myself eligible for the draft. Had a ring and everything. As soon as I got drafted I was going to propose to her."

There's a churning in my gut. The only way this can end is bad, and I feel awful for Cutter because I have a feeling this broke his young heart.

"The summer was on us, and I'd invited Ransom down to help me move. There was some of Katie's stuff in my dorm. I wasn't sure when we'd get to see each other. She was going home to Tennessee for a while, and I wanted her to have it if she needed it. We packed it up, and I let myself into her apartment using the key she gave me."

I reach over, grasping his hand in mine, gripping his fingers because I can tell this isn't going to be good. The way his voice has thinned, the way he's pushing forward not wanting it to stop.

"She was fuckin' another guy in her bed. He had her bent over, pounding her from behind, and he was saying all kinds of shit. Telling her to tell him who she really loved, asking her why she was with me, and she would groan out because the coach is paying me to keep him happy."

Tears spring to my eyes as I think of the young kid

Cutter used to be, giving his heart to a woman he thought he'd love forever, learning in such a crass way that she didn't care for him at all.

"I lost it. I pulled the guy off her and beat the living shit out of him. The whole time words were flying out of my mouth, to this day I don't remember what I said. The only reason I stopped was because she'd run buck-ass-naked out of the room and gotten Ransom to get me off the guy."

"Oh, Cutter..."

"I went to the coach and asked him if what she'd said was true. He admitted it, especially after I got picked up for beating the guy. It came out internally, but stayed out of the press that I'd accepted bribes I didn't know were bribes. I lost my scholarship and after that, football left a bad taste in my mouth. I can't even really watch it these days," he sighs.

"I'm sorry that happened to you."

"I grew from it." He gives me a sad smile. "But it's always made me cautious when it comes to women, which is why I'm scared to death to tell you how I feel about you."

"You don't have to be scared." I lean in, kissing him softly on the lips.

He holds my neck, keeping us close together. I can feel the whispered breath on my mouth. "Then if I told you I love you, would you run?"

My pulse vibrates in my wrist. I shake my head. "No, I would tell you that through all the crazy shit we've been through, I love you too."

CHAPTER TWENTY-FIVE

Cutter

"YOU DO?"

I can't believe what I'm hearing. It was the absolute last thing I expected.

"Yeah." She grins. "I haven't let myself feel this way in a long time, but with you, it's natural."

That's exactly how it feels for me too. Completely natural.

I go to wrap my arms around her, but she shrinks back. "If you've been honest with me, I need to be honest with you."

"You don't have to tell me anything," I assure her. "Me confiding in you was something I needed to do."

She reaches over, grabbing my beer, taking a drink of it. "I need to confide in you, too."

"Then please, I'm here to listen to you. I'm here to help you through anything. I won't judge."

Relief flashes in her blue eyes. "Thank you."

"No need to thank me."

She sits back against the outdoor fabric, looking like the life has completely deflated from her body. "This is so hard." Her voice shakes. "I've never told anyone about this. Since I've always lived in Paradise Lost, everyone knows. The only people I've talked to about it are medical professionals."

Now I'm getting a little worried. Not for me, but for her. Obviously this is something much more serious than I assumed it would be.

"You can tell me anything." I grab her hand, bringing the back of it up to my lips, hoping this little gesture will be enough for her to know I'm here.

"When I was seventeen, I got pregnant." She pushes the words out of her mouth on a long sigh. "It was totally unplanned, I was on birth control. We'd been having sex for over a year."

"So you had a long-term boyfriend?"

"Tommie. He was two years older than me, and he was friends with my brothers before we started dating." She gets a faraway look on her face. "He was tall, strong, and everything a teenage girl wants in her first real boyfriend. He paid attention to me, told me I was pretty, and went out of his way to tell my brothers off when they'd make fun of us." She turns so that she can sit cross-legged, propping her chin up on our hands.

"Graduation night, he'd rented us a hotel room so we could be together all night. My parents thought I was staying with friends. That's the night I got pregnant. The night my life completely changed."

Why do I feel like this story is going to kill me? Chew me up and spit me out?

"My parents, being old-fashioned believed Tommie and

I should've gotten married. So we did. They signed for me since I wasn't yet eighteen, and we moved into this little trailer on the outskirts of Paradise Lost."

"At seventeen you were a wife?"

"Yeah, it was real weird going from cooking yourself mac and cheese for dinner to cooking an entire meal for your husband. Tommie was getting his EMT Certification, and I helped him study. It seemed interesting to me, and I knew I wanted to do it too. We got grants because we were young, married, and I was pregnant. He graduated the program right before I gave birth, and I entered the program when I was twelve weeks pregnant."

"To be so young." I caress her face. "The two of you were doing amazing things."

"We thought so." She smiles sadly. "We'd managed to graduate without student loan debt, we worked on a shoestring budget, and we were doing the best we could to provide for Etta."

"Etta?" I ask, somehow knowing that was their baby.

"Yeah." Her eyes shine brightly with unshed tears. "I named her after the Jazz singer. I loved going to News Orleans and listening to Jazz, it was one of my favorite things to do. When we found out we were having a girl, it was the only thing I could think of. Her name had to be Etta."

She reaches into her pocket for her phone, scrolling for a few minutes. When she finally finds what she wants, she proudly shows a picture of a very young Rowan holding a toddler who looks to be about the same age as Keegan.

"Rowan, she's the spitting image of you. She's beautiful."

"Yeah." Rowan pulls her bottom lip in between her teeth before she licks at her upper one, taking some of her tears with her. "She was my best friend, which is weird to say because she was so young, but we were growing up together."

"How as it going with Tommie?"

Her shrug tells me everything I need to know. "He wasn't adjusting as well as I was. He wanted to go out with his friends and do the fun things he'd been able to before, but we were working on opposing shifts so we didn't have to afford childcare. I found out later he felt trapped, which was what lead to him drinking more than normal."

This breaks my heart for her. She and her daughter should have been loved, they should have been cared for, not made to feel like they were a burden. The man lucky enough to have them should have known how blessed he was. "Did he hurt you?" I'm scared to ask, but I need to know.

"Not physically." Her chin trembles, and I want with everything I am to reach over and make it strong again, but I know she has to do this on her own. "Once we started working full-time, the both of us, it was good money. Money we weren't used to, so we were able to do things many other people our age wouldn't have been. Because we were so used to living on not much money, we continued to do it for a year and a half. Soon, we had enough money for a down-payment on a house. It was a brand-new subdivision, big lots with pools in the backyard. I was nervous about the pool, but everyone said 'Rowan, you've worked hard, you deserve to have what you want.' I believed them."

An ache starts in the back of my throat as I mentally try to prepare myself for what she may say. All signs are pointing to something horrible happening to her kid. "Take your time."

I'm sure I say the words for not only her, but me. I feel as if I need to be eased into whatever happened. I'm as emotionally invested as she is. She takes a breath I feel to my soul and soldiers on.

"He was supposed to be watching her, just like he always did, but we'd been arguing. He wasn't happy with our relationship and I wasn't happy with the lack of effort he was putting forth. We'd been married for almost five years, and we were both getting older, growing up, and wanting different things. For me, Etta was my world, and for Tommie, she was a bump in the road and she was holding him back. He'd admitted that to me a few days before. I'd gotten home and he'd been drinking. We argued about being married at our age, and I'd asked if he wanted a divorce. He said no because it'd disappoint his parents," she snorts.

"Tommie sounds like a real winner."

Her eyes cut to me and the sorrow in them is so sharp it slices me like a knife. "When I got home that day, Tommie was inside, and I knew, I knew something was wrong. I yelled to him, asking where Etta was. He said she was out back, but he'd locked the gate." She shakes her head. "That was one thing he never did. He never checked it. I looked over at him and he was holding a beer in his hand. He'd obviously come inside to get it, leaving our four-year-old outside. Alone. I ran out, screaming her name. As soon as I got to the gate, I could see her, her dark hair floating in the water. She was face-down."

"Jesus." I'm pushing the tears in my eyes back. This is her story, these are her feelings, and I need to let her have them. I never even knew Etta.

"I yelled for him to call 911, before I dove into the pool. When I got out with her, he was still standing there. Our neighbor heard me screaming and called 911. I did CPR on her until the other paramedics got there, begging him to help me, but he just watched. Like he was in a daze, and all I could think was this is what he wanted. A clean slate for his life to go back the way it was."

"Do you really believe that?" Because I can't imagine someone wanting their child dead.

"He never refuted it. Not when I called him out during my counseling sessions after I had a nervous breakdown, and not during the divorce."

"God, Rowan, I'm so sorry."

She wipes tears from her face. "It's made me stronger. I'm much more aware of my mental health, and I've kept to myself since all this happened. I spent six-months in an in-patient rehab getting my life back together, and he just went on like nothing happened. I hate him and I don't think anyone will ever be able to convince me otherwise."

Wrapping my arms around her, I hold her tight, rocking her back and forth, whispering promises into her ear. I promise to never be like her ex-husband and pray to God I'll never disappoint her in the ways he did.

CHAPTER TWENTY-SIX

Rowan

"THIS IS SO CUTE!"

I love the downtown look of Laurel Springs. We're in Cutter's truck driving to The Café, where we're having breakfast with his family. I'm doing my best to not be sad because I have to leave tonight, but I'm thankful for the time we've gotten to spend together.

"Yeah, it is. You know, it's funny. I've spent most of my life wondering why I can't get out of this town, but now that I've been to Paradise Lost and Tuscaloosa, I realize how much I love it here. We have a hometown vibe not many get to have."

I could see myself living here. I don't say the words out loud, but I could. The feel of the place is so happy. There aren't bad memories everywhere I turn. There's just a chance to make new ones.

He turns on his blinker, groaning. "Looks like everybody and their mama's here today."

"What do you mean?" But then I see it, a huge row of cars, trucks, and a couple of Jeeps.

"Mom must have invited the entire LSERT to eat this morning. Don't touch that door," he says when he parks, shutting the truck off.

I smile at him as he jogs around the front end, coming over to open my door. He helps me down, and then holding my hand, we walk to the entrance of The Café. There's a sign on the door proclaiming it's closed for a private party. He groans again.

It makes me laugh, and I smack him in the stomach. "It's not that big of a deal, I think it's sweet that everybody cares enough about you to check me out."

"I do too," he admits. "Especially after Katie. I really do have the best family."

He does, and as I walk into the welcoming faces, I can't help but want to be a part of it in the worst way. It's a physical ache that starts in my stomach and works up to my chest, a warmth I haven't felt in so, so long. At home I feel like I can't be myself, not with everyone knowing about what I've done, and what's happened to me. Here they don't have preconceived notions. They get to see the new me, the real me I've fostered through years of therapy and a whole lot of willpower.

The faces are a blur as I'm introduced to a lot of people, in addition to the ones I met yesterday. Given the way everyone looks at Cutter with pride in their eyes, they're happy for him. Obviously he sees himself in a completely different way than the people in his life see him. Immediately I wonder if I'm doing the same thing. Can I not get beyond how people looked at me when I came back to work after my breakdown?

His family has saved us a seat at a large round table, but really it seems as if everyone is family. There are men and women, kids, a few dogs, and they're all yelling from table to table. I haven't been in a situation like this where I've felt comfortable in years. It always feels like everyone is looking at me, wondering when I'm about to break.

Cutter pulls my seat out for me and motions for me to sit down. I do, only to realize I'm next to Stella. "You're not gonna kill me, are you?"

She laughs, throwing her head back. "No, I'm not going to kill you, we just won't ever be able to watch a college football game together, and during the Iron Bowl, please forgive me for anything I say." She holds out her hand for a shake.

"Deal."

The longer I'm there, the better I feel. Holden has pulled me into a conversation about my dad. "I semi-retired a few years ago, I want to retire fully, but I'm not sure I'll ever be able to really do it. Once you're used to police work and it's in your blood, it's hard to let go."

"That and he just likes bossing people around." Leigh places a kiss on the top of his head as she puts some plates down on the table. "Stella, can you come help me grab the rest of this? That way we'll all be able to eat together."

She stands up, looks around, her gaze eventually landing on me, without a second thought she shoves Keegan into my arms. "Can you hold him for a few minutes? If we let him down he'll start playing with the pups and then I'll have to wash his hands again. Thank you!"

Before I can say anything or even react, I'm holding Keegan. This is the first child I've held since Etta, and I'm hit with an emotion I never thought I'd have again - contentment. "Hey." I bounce him on my lap. "Remember me? I'm Rowan."

He giggles, leaning forward, taking my cheeks in his hands, and then he drops a sticky kiss on my nose. It's so unexpected, but I giggle along with him, so happy I can have this moment. Cutter sits down next to us, reaching in to tickle his nephew on his stomach.

"What do you think you're doing, Keeg? Moving in on my girl?"

Keegan reaches for his uncle, and I reluctantly give him up, trying to tell my heart not to skip too many beats now that Cutter's proclaimed me his girl. The independent woman I've been for the last few years should rally against it, should hate that he's taking slight ownership of me, but I like it. I want to be his, I want him to be mine, and if at all possible, I want to be a part of this amazing family. They've shown me my smile again. One I thought I'd lost forever. A small-town in Northern Alabama has taught me it's okay to move on, and finally, I feel like I can.

"I CAN'T BELIEVE you already have to leave." Cutter kicks at the rocks on the ground. We're standing in front of his parents' house, where we've been watching movies all afternoon with his brother's family and his parents. I wasn't sure how I would feel, but they welcomed me with open arms.

Being with all of them is easier than being with my family. With everything they've seen me deal with, at my lowest point ever, and me being ashamed of it. Our relationship has never been the same, and it's not because of them. It's because of me.

"I know, but I've gotta be at work at six a.m." I wrap my arms around his neck. "Maybe you can come see me?"

"We get our schedule in the next few days. I hope I'll be able to work it out."

"So we're really gonna be able to do this?" I ask, standing on tiptoe and sneaking in a kiss. "Will we be able to do this long-distance thing?"

"I'm committed if you are." He holds me tightly. "You fit perfectly in with my life, Ro, I've waited years to find a woman like you."

"Ditto, Cutter."

My watch beeps, letting me know another hour has passed. It's another hour that I should have already been on the road, but I've ignored it for as long as I can.

"I know, you've got to leave." He tightens his arms around me. "I wish you didn't have to."

I wish I didn't either, but I'm not sure I can say those words to him right now, I'm too emotional. This trip has made me realize what all I'm missing in my life, and shown me I can have it right here.

"Call me when you get there and if you stop," he whispers, kissing my neck. "Love you."

I smile widely. "Love you, too."

Always the gentleman, he opens my door, helps me in, and watches as I back out of the driveway. Even in the darkness, I can see him thanks to the motion-detector light on the side of the house, walking down the driveway to watch me as I roll down the street. I get to the stop sign, and there's an alert from my phone, letting me know I have a text message.

Reaching over, I grab it, seeing that it's coming from Cutter. Since I'm already at the stop sign, I give myself a few moments, open the message, and sob like the emotional woman I am.

He's sent me a picture of me and Keegan, right when Keegan reached in to give me that kiss. Downloading and saving it to my phone, I feel a piece of my broken heart slide back together. It isn't fully intact yet, but it's getting there, and I have a feeling this town, these people, they are going to be my road to happiness. They are going to pull me out from under this dark cloud following me around.

The only question is, am I strong enough to do what I feel? Am I strong enough to possibly leave my family and start a life in a place where the only person I really know is a man who's told me he loves me after a few weeks?

I'm still undecided, but leaning more toward yes.

After all, I got married at seventeen, had a baby, lost a baby, lost a marriage, and I've come out the other side. If this doesn't work out, it won't break me.

It might very well kill me, but I know I won't let it break me.

I've already been broken and I refuse to fall apart again.

CHAPTER TWENTY-SEVEN

Cutter

"IS THIS THE FOR-SURE SCHEDULE?" I ask my supervisor as I take a look at what our next two weeks look like on the rotation.

"Yeah, I gave you four days off in a row after being down at Paradise Lost. I figured you could use it."

"Thanks." I grin at him, already pulling my phone out of my pocket.

Four days off in a row? That means I can head down there if I want to and spend some more time with Rowan. She may not be off, but at least I can be there when she is, and we can continue to get to know one another better.

C: Guess what? I got the lucky shift and I'm off four days in a row after today. I can leave around eight tonight, if you're willing to put me up?

It doesn't even take two minutes for her to answer.

R: OMG! YES! Come down here. I get off work at six, so that's perfect. I can't wait to see you, even though it's only been two days.
C: Same, I was missing you in my bed more than I wanted to admit.
R: We're about to go on a run, but I'll see you when you get here. Love you, Cutter.
C: Love you, too.

The newness of this hasn't worn off yet, I still get little pricks of excitement in my stomach when she says she loves me. I hope it never goes away. More than anything I want to be like my parents and the other guys in the LSERT, those that have found love and will do anything to protect it. *At all costs* is their favorite motto, and I can see why now that I have Rowan in my life.

"Got big plans?" Devante, a new recruit from Atlanta, asks as I get into the ambulance beside him. "Saw you got four days off in a row, you lucky fuck."

I grin over at him. I like him a lot and hope he stays. "Sometimes you win, sometimes you lose, right now I'm on a winning streak."

"Oh get outta here with that, they're just trying to kiss your ass 'cause you volunteered to go to Paradise Lost."

"That ain't a lie. You coulda volunteered," I point out.

"Not a member of the LSERT." He checks the blind spot as we drive around, waiting for a call.

"You could be."

"Do they take new people?"

"Hell yeah." I'm confused as to why he wouldn't think we'd take him. "Shelby, the attorney who helped Tucker and Karsyn? She just signed up for legal advocacy if it's needed. We'd love to have you, man."

"It's just been so weird," he continues. "Moving here for this job. Coming from a town like Atlanta where there's a definitely an integrated population, and then coming here."

Now I get what he's saying. As one of the only African American members in any of our first responder branches, he's got to be feeling slightly left out. "I'm not gonna pretend like I know how you feel," I start, wondering if I wanna go down this road. "Because I've always had family around, I've never been a minority and I've never had to wonder, but I will say the people on this team are some of the best people I know. We would benefit greatly from your expertise, and there is a population of this town who feels as if they aren't served. You could reach them much better than we can. No offense to you."

"None taken." He looks at me, his brows pulled together in a shrewd stare. "You've made a good case, Cutter. I might check it out."

"Do," I encourage him. "If it's not for you, then it's not for you, but at least give it a shot before you decide. If you're not comfortable checking it out on your own, I'll take you. I got people," I laugh.

"You sure do, like the whole fuckin' police department and half the rest of the town."

"I can't help it that my family is huge."

"Heard you had a woman from Paradise Lost came up to see you." He wiggles his eyebrows at me.

Gossip in the EMT community runs as rampant as it does in the police department. "I did, she's a fellow first responder, I met her on the job down there."

"That's nice, at least she's someone who understands when work runs over and you can't make the date, or you're late for dinner. It's hard to find women who are understanding in situations like that."

"You sound like you speak from experience."

"There's a reason I came here from Atlanta, and it most definitely wasn't the damn signing bonus."

I want to ask more, but we aren't that close yet. I don't want to pry, even though I want to know what happened. He deserves respect and to open up when he feels it's the proper thing to do.

Our radio goes off, mentioning our ambulance number. I reach over, answering the call.

"Go on."

"We've got an older gentleman with flu-like symptoms."

They rattle off the address, and we're heading to the scene. Devante is still unsure of most of the roads here, so when he goes to make a turn that will take us longer, I stop him.

"If you go farther up the road, turn to the left, and then immediately to the right, we'll take a back alley that'll get us there quicker."

"Got it." He puts the pedal down, both of us feeling the adrenaline in our bodies. My foot is beating a tattoo on the floor and he's got one hand drumming the steering wheel.

"You see him?" I ask as we pull up to the residence.

"He must be inside."

We get our stretcher out, as well as our emergency bags, and head up to the front door.

"Hey, my man," I say as I go inside. "You feel bad? What's hurting?"

The man answers. "Everything."

"Let's get you to the front door so we can get you on a stretcher."

We help him out and as we get him on the bed, I look over at Devante. "He's struggling to breathe, this doesn't look like the flu."

"Looks tachy," Devante says as we get him into the back.

"Then we need to get moving, you drive and I'll handle this."

Quickly, he helps me get the patient situated and then goes to the front of the ambulance, and off we go. I'm running a machine on him and see that his heart rate is almost two-hundred. "You got heart problems?"

"Not that I know of."

There are two things I can do in this situation: give him medicine to bring his heart rate down, or use pads to shock it back into rhythm. The first thing we always try is the medicine.

"You feeling alright?"

"I hurt all over."

When I run another report, I see that his heart rate isn't down any lower than it was to begin with. I'm going to have to hit him with the pads. I get on the radio, calling up the Emergency Room.

"I'm going to use the paddles, but his heart rate doesn't seem to be coming down yet, be prepared for us."

"You're gonna feel like you've been punched in the chest," I warn him. "But this is what we need to do, to make sure we get you better. We've got to get you out of this heart rate as soon as we can."

"Okay," he gasps. "Do what you have to."

I can see the fear in his eyes and this is where I wish I could take all the fear away from my patients. I'm only with them for a short period of time, but I don't want them to be afraid. "Here we go."

He screams as he's shocked with fifty joules of electricity, but I can immediately see his heart rate is starting to slow. "I think that did it."

I radio to the hospital letting them know the heart rate is starting to come down, proud that I've been able to help this man, even if I had to hurt to help. We pull into the hospital, transferring his care off to the Emergency Room doctors. It's always hard to watch your patient leave and not know the outcome. It's human nature to want to see it through to the end, but we can't.

Me and Devante hop back into our ambulance and go about finishing our shift.

"Three hours to go." I glance at my watch, mentally counting down how much longer it'll be until I can leave.

"You're pitiful," he laughs, as he checks both the left and the right before proceeding to pull out of the parking lot.

"I accept that."

People can make fun of me all day long, I don't care. I finally have the woman I've always dreamed about, the life I've always wanted, and I'm being seen as a mature adult who can take care of himself. For so long I've fought the image of teenage Cutter everyone had.

Now is my time to shine, now it's time for me to get out from under what's been holding me down, and the person who's bringing this all out in me is hours away.

But I'm only hours from seeing her and knowing that

will help me get through the rest of this day. Soon I'll have Laurel Springs in my rearview and Paradise Lost in my sights.

CHAPTER TWENTY-EIGHT

Rowan

THE KNOCK on my door causes me to shriek in excitement. I know it's Cutter, and even though it's only been a few days, I've missed him. I run so fast I slide on the hardwood, hitting the door in the front foyer. "Ouch."

"Ro, are you okay?"

I'm holding my forehead as I swing it open, and let him in. "Fine, I was too excited and skid."

He sweeps me up in his arms, and I'm back where I've wanted to be since I left Laurel Springs. "Missed you." He runs his nose along my jawline.

"Missed you, too."

This time I release him from my grip, letting him come completely into the living room. "Four days, huh?"

"Four days," he confirms, excitement in his eyes.

But I can see it, the weariness marked by dark circles. "How long have you been awake?"

He glances at his watch. "Going on twenty hours."

"As excited as I am that you're here, I really think you should get some sleep. It'll won't do either of us any good if you're dead on your feet."

"But you work tomorrow," he argues.

"Which means you can sleep as long as you want."

He nods, appearing almost thankful. He gets undressed, slipping under the covers with me. Together we lie down in my bed, our arms wrapped tightly around one another.

It'll be the best sleep I've gotten in days.

THE NEXT MORNING, I do my best not to wake him up, but he stirs as I get dressed.

"Ro?" His voice is thick with sleep, the way I love hearing it.

"Go back to sleep." I bend down, kissing him on the forehead. "I'll see you when I get off work. I'm changing my schedule around so I'm off tomorrow and we'll be able to hang out all day."

"Okay." He drops back down on the pillow, holding the one I had been sleeping on in his arms. Judging by his even breathing, he's out before I even get up from the bed.

This could be my life. If I were strong enough to take it and hold on with two hands. I'm scared I won't be, but I know I want it. Want it more than anything I've ever wanted besides Etta being back in our lives.

There's one person I need to talk to though, the one who will give me the lowdown on how I'm feeling. The one who won't sugarcoat anything. Dragging my cellphone over to me, I shoot off a text to Sullivan, asking for lunch.

When he answers back that he'd love to, I feel better

than I have in a long time.

It feels like it takes forever to get to lunch, I want to talk to Sullivan that badly. When it's finally lunch hour, I wave Isaac off, I tell him I'm going to eat with my brother and ask him to drop me at a local park. When we get there, Sullivan is already at a picnic table with our food.

"To what do I owe the pleasure of lunch with you?"

He's joking, we have lunch together all the time, but for some reason those words bring tears to my eyes.

"Hey, what's going on?"

I struggle, not sure how I want to tell him how I'm feeling. I don't want to come across as rude, or like I don't appreciate what people have done for me.

"I'm suffocating," I start.

"Do you need me to call Isaac back here?" His eyes are wide and full of fear.

"No, not like that," I laugh. "This place, Paradise Lost, it's suffocating me. Everywhere I look there are memories. Good, but bad too, and some I'll never be able to get over."

He relaxes and takes a drink of the milkshake he got. "So what does that mean?"

"You know I went to visit Cutter the other day?"

"Yeah." He nods. "Dad thought it was crazy, Mom wished you well, and Braylon didn't give a shit."

"What did you think?" I study him closely. The two of us have always been the closest and his response will mean everything to me.

"I envy you," he finally pushes out. "The fact that you're able to go somewhere else."

"Do you feel suffocated too?"

"Yeah." He runs a hand through his hair. It's getting longer and dad's been on him to get it cut. "Like I'm supposed to stay here and take over Dad's spot, I'm supposed to keep chasing the same woman who wants abso-fuckin-lutely nothing to do with me. It's almost like we're not able to spread our wings and find out what else is out there. More than anything I want to be happy with what I'm doing every day, but there are so many preconceived notions about us here."

"Right? You get what I'm saying. If Cutter asks me, I'm moving to Laurel Springs."

All last night while he slept next to me I thought about it, and there's really one answer. To go, to leave all this behind and make a fresh start.

"Are you sure that's a good idea?"

Sully's always the voice of reason, always the person who knows we should think through everything we're going to do.

"You'll be leaving Etta here."

"Maybe that's the point." I run my hand along the back of my neck. "I love her desperately, but I need to let her go. Forever she'll be stuck as a four-year-old in my mind and I refuse to see her as anything different. I think maybe I'm keeping myself stuck here because I don't know how to move on. It can't be healthy."

"How would you feel with no family around?" He raises an eyebrow.

This is another question I've given a lot of thought and now's the time to play my Ace. "I know you, bro. I know you're not happy here. You just told me you feel suffocated. Come with me, I'm sure the Laurel Springs PD would appreciate your expertise."

"It's a tough decision." He takes a bite of his food, while I chew mine. "Dad would be disappointed."

I roll my eyes. "When is Dad not disappointed?"

We share a look and then laugh. It's the truth, he always wants the best for all of us, but what's best is his definition. Not ours.

"Let me think about it."

"Take all the time you need, Cutter's not anywhere near asking me, I'm sure. Who knows if he even will, this may be something I have to decide to do on my own."

"I'm sure he's going to ask you, I've seen the way he looks at you. It's the way you deserve to be looked at."

That warms my chest, makes me happy to have a brother whose so supportive of me and everything I've ever wanted to do. "You'll have it too, Sully."

"Maybe."

But I can tell by the way he speaks he doesn't believe it.

"I promise."

"Don't make promises you can't keep, sis."

"Touché."

We finish our lunch in relative silence, neither one of us wanting to admit we're not sure what to say or what to do. We both have some really big decisions to make, and they won't be easy, but I hope they'll be worth it.

A few minutes later, Isaac turns in to pick me up. Sully grabs our stuff, throwing it away before he walks me to the ambulance. Once there he hugs me tight.

"You're shining, Ro. Whatever it is he's doing, he's doing it right."

"Which is why I want you with me." I hug him tighter. "You always told me I needed a better man than Tommie. I got one, and I want you to see how he treats me. This is everything you always wanted for me."

He lets go, opening the door for me.

"Hey." He waves to Isaac. "Y'all stay safe out here."

Isaac waves back. "You too."

When Sully shuts my door, Isaac looks over at me. "You're leaving, aren't you?"

I shouldn't be surprised. He's known everything about me since we started being partners. There's not been one thing I've been able to hide from him, even when I wanted to.

"I'm leaving." I nod, sure of it now that I've talked to Sullivan.

"I'm gonna miss you." Issac puts his sunglasses down over his eyes, and if I'm not mistaken he's hiding the emotions he's feeling.

"I'm gonna miss you too, I'm gonna miss it here."

I can't lie, this has been my home since I was born, there will be things I won't be able to get anywhere else, but change can be good and I feel like I'm ready for one. In fact I know I'm ready for one.

The stupid thing to do would be to keep moving in the same direction I've been moving in and then wonder why there isn't an improvement in my life. If I want one, I have to make it happen, and this golden opportunity has been laid in my lap. I must take it, I'm not sure when I'll have another one.

"But I've been living in the past for too long," I continue. "The past is keeping me from having a future, and it's making my present worse."

"Then you've definitely got to make a change," Isaac agrees. "If anyone deserves to be happy, it's you, and only you can make that decision for yourself."

As we leave the park, I'm ninety-nine percent sure I've made up my mind. Now all I have to do is figure out how I'm going to execute this life change.

CHAPTER TWENTY-NINE

Cutter

GOING to the beach is something different for me. We went sometimes when I was little, but it was hard with Mom always working at The Café. I, of course, did the whole Spring Break experience, but it's not the same as coming with Rowan.

"We'll park in the EMT lot." She winks as she turns her car in, displaying her badge. "It's almost ten bucks an hour to park in the public lots. Everybody who works here does it."

"Little rule breaker," I joke as she parks in one of the back spaces.

"Sometimes rules are meant to be broken."

This is a side of her I like. One where she's not so completely worried about what other people think of her. It's cute and sexy. We get out, grabbing our stuff out of the trunk.

"How long has it been since you've been to the beach to

have fun?" she asks as we walk across the street onto the public part of the sand.

"Not since you swallowed for me there a few days ago," I laugh as her eyes grow big and she busts out laughing.

"Cutter!"

"Kidding, it's been a while. Like since Spring Break my freshman year of college."

"I'm sure not much has changed, you've just gotten older."

"Look at you with the jokes."

We find a spot to lay our stuff, and then I watch as she shrugs out of her t-shirt and shorts. I'm not sure what I expected, but what I get is so far out of my wildest dreams, I'm flabbergasted. She's wearing a one-piece with one side cut-out and it's giving me ideas.

"Holy fuck, Ro."

"I bought it last year." She grins. "And I've not had a chance to wear it yet. I thought I'd wear it for you."

Knowing she's wearing something from me is giving me a semi. "Let's get in the water."

We grab hands, running down to the edge, not stopping until I'm thigh deep in the foamy surf. It's up to her chest and she reaches up, grabbing hold of me. Her thighs are wrapped around my waist and my hands are supporting her as she leans back, dipping her hair into the water. It's down today; I decided not to make a big deal about it, but I wanted to.

For at least an hour, we play in the water, swimming out and coming back in. I pick her up and throw her, she swims out of my range and teases me by slyly pushing one of the shoulder straps down.

"Stop," I laugh. "You're gonna get something you can't handle."

"I'm pretty sure I've proven to you I can handle it."

When the sun is high in the sky, she looks at me. "I don't know about you, but I'm hungry. Let's walk down the pier and get some lunch."

We leave our towels on the beach, but put our coverups back on and walk hand-in-hand along the shoreline. There are families and kids running past us. When we're almost to the pier a football lands at our feet.

"Sorry!" some kids yell. "Can you throw it back to us?"

"Yeah, Mr. College Football Player. Throw it back to them."

I put more heat on it than I should. When the kid catches, he asks if I'll throw back and forth with them. "You throw better than my brother," he whines.

"Sorry, I'm going to get some lunch." I point up to the pier. "Maybe some other time."

Putting my arm around Rowan's neck, I guide her up the stairs.

"I think you broke that kid's heart."

"Then I'm a first in a long line - he's got to get used to it."

She giggles. "You're harsh."

"Life isn't all fairytales and marshmallows."

"Marshmallows? Where did that even come from?" She snorts.

I point over to one of the booths that proclaims it's selling s'mores. "They're my favorite treat."

We head on over to the booth, purchase corn dogs, fries to share, and the s'mores treat I'm not sure I can leave here without trying. We get a seat in the shade and listen to the waves as they beat the sand.

"This is almost the perfect day." Ro stretches.

"Almost?"

"Only thing that would make it better would be a beer in my hand, but alcohol isn't allowed out here."

She's got a point, but I'd say it's pretty perfect being here with her. We're lazy as we eat our food.

"I wish we had a place like this in Laurel Springs."

"No you don't." She shakes her head. "It's crowded in the summer and fall. Vacationers are the worst kinds of people, they always do something to disturb the ecosystem around them. I wish we weren't so well known."

"That's fair."

"Let's walk some of this off," she suggests, nodding toward the end of the pier where there are a few shops and some game booths set up.

It doesn't take long for us to get there, and when we do, she pulls me into a photo booth. "Let's take our picture."

I reach out, putting some money into the slot before I have a seat and pull her on my lap.

"Smile," she instructs, so I put my chin on her shoulder and smile brightly as the picture is taken.

"Goofy," I say this time, sticking my tongue out and crossing my eyes.

"Serious," she giggles.

"You won't get serious if you're laughing."

She looks at me and I look at her. The moment is perfect as she tilts her head to the side for a kiss. We hear the picture get taken right as I'm shoving my tongue in her mouth, trying to see how far she'll let me take this.

My hand moves up her shirt, cupping her breast through her swimsuit. Unabashedly my thumb runs over her nipple, groaning when I feel it spring to life. I've never been with a woman who is as responsive as her, and I'm obsessed. Literally addicted to the way she makes me feel.

Someone knocks on the side of the booth. "Are you done in there yet?"

I groan, whispering in her ear. "Guess we are now."

Both of us try to make ourselves presentable as we exit. "Sorry," she apologizes. "We thought we had a couple more pictures to take."

The knowing look from the male in this couple lets me know he is completely on to us. We snatch our pictures up before walking farther down the pier. There's a bunch of games set up, proclaiming you can win stuffed animals or even money.

"You want me to win you something?"

She pinches at my waist. "You think you can? There's nothing less attractive than a man who thinks he's hot stuff and then can't deliver."

"Oh I can assure you I deliver every single time."

We both know we aren't talking about these games, but it's fun to play with her. I've never had this kind of teasing relationship. It's one I've watched my parents and my brother have. I always wondered what it would feel like.

Happiness.

I'm happier than I've ever been.

Which scares the fuck out of me, but as Dad said, love is scary. It's the great unknown and the world's biggest gut-check.

We stop at the water balloon booth.

"Step right up. You get five darts for three dollars. You get a gift for every balloon popped, or you can trade it in for a bigger gift."

"See anything you like?"

I watch Rowan eye everything in the booth, wondering what the hell she's going to pick. A lot of it looks cheap, but it could have sentimental value of our day together, of this time in our new relationship. "That bear over there." She points. "Wearing the Paradise Lost Beach t-shirt. Win me him."

"You heard the lady." I pluck down ten bucks, in all honestly not sure of how my skills will match up to this totally rigged game.

The first one hits the balloon but doesn't bust it.

"Oh come on."

This happens for two more, and then I'm pissed. Ro stands at my side giving me encouragement, but it's not doing a whole hell of a lot when, even though my darts are hitting the balloons, nothing is happening.

"Dude, you rigged the fuck out of this game."

The operator doesn't say anything - he doesn't have to. I'm the idiot who decided to show off in front of my girlfriend.

"If you can get this done," Ro whispers in my ear. "I'll reward you very well tonight. Think of our first night together."

All I can think of is the blow job she gave me and how it blew my mind. It's more than enough incentive for me to throw the darts harder, somehow pressing against the balloons. When I finally have what I need to get her the bear she wants, I look triumphantly at the operator. "Give her the bear."

He grumbles, she squeals in excitement, and I just hope no one can tell what she's promised me.

Grabbing her hand, we lazily stroll down the rest of the pier before going back to our towels in the sand.

"I'm so tired," she yawns. "Something about the water and the food."

I get us a couple of umbrellas and together, tired and our bellies full, we take a nap in the sand with the ocean and chattering families as our background noise.

If anyone were to ask me, I would tell them this is the perfect day, and it's a memory I'll hold onto forever.

Looking over at Rowan, I send a little thanks up that she came into my life at the most unexpected time.

CHAPTER THIRTY

Rowan

IT'S BEEN A LONG, but good day when Cutter and I decide it's time to leave. My face is slightly tight, meaning I'm probably sunburned. I hope not badly considering we applied sunscreen every few hours.

As we walk back across the street and into the parking lot, he holds my hand, swinging our entwined fingers between us. It's one of the cutest things he's ever done.

We're approaching where I parked, so I reluctantly let go.

Reaching into my beach bag to fish out my keys, I point over to where my car is parked, only to let an oath out of my mouth. "Fuck me."

"Excuse me?"

"Not what I meant to say. It's just..." There's a man leaning beside my car. He's one I avoid at all costs, but every once in a while he'll corner me, want to talk to me in a public setting where he knows I won't make a scene. "I don't want to see him right now."

"Who is he?" Cutter asks.

The man standing beside my car hears him, and together the two of us answer, our voices raising to be the one heard. It all comes out in a jumble, and as Cutter hears, he looks like he wants to bolt.

"Her husband."

"My *ex*-husband."

Cutter

MY STOMACH CLENCHES as I hear "her husband". Even though she's said ex, immediately I'm taken back to college.

"Your husband?" I turn to her. She knows my history, knows it wasn't easy to talk about it, and still she didn't tell me this. Did she lie to me? Are they not really divorced?

"No." She shakes her head, reaching out to grab my wrist. "I didn't lie to you," she knows exactly where my head is. "Not my husband."

I look at the man standing in front of me, he's wearing an EMT uniform, a sleeve of tattoos running down his arm. "Do you have a thing for EMT's with tattoos?" I sneer, not able to keep the venom out of my voice.

"What?" She straightens her back. "Are you serious right now?"

"Are you?"

My heart is pounding, I'm gasping for breath, trying to keep myself upright. Not even in college did I feel this amount of betrayal. I hadn't given myself to that girl, not like

I thought I had. But Rowan, I gave myself to her. Every single bit, and I hadn't even thought twice about it. The feelings just happened, and I'd allowed it.

Stupid fucker.

"Cutter, snap out of it, remember I told you." She grabs my face in both her hands, forcing me to look at her. "Remember, I hate him. He got the tattoos after we got divorced."

"You don't hate me." The guy walks forward, reaching out to grab Rowan's wrist.

That puts everything back into perspective for me. I knock his hand down, the dark rage leaving my vision. I'm more level-headed than I was and I feel the panic pushing down in my chest. "She divorced you, you don't get to touch her."

Rowan makes a noise of relief in her throat.

"What the fuck do you even know about us, dude?"

This guy is going to regret talking to me like that. "I'm not your dude, and she told me everything I need to know about you, man. Who sits on the sidelines and watches as their wife tries to save their child? Who doesn't rise to the occasion and help? Are you even a man?"

His eyes flash and in my periphery, I can see his hands ball into fists. "You bow up on me bro, and you better be able to knock me down with the first punch. I will destroy you."

Rowan tries to get in the middle of us. "Cutter, he isn't worth it."

"No," Tommie says. "*He* isn't worth it. He'll get sick of you just like I did. He'll want a different life. Not to be nagged all the fuckin' time about where he is. Forced to pretend like you have the perfect family."

"Screw you." Rowan turns on him, putting her finger to

his chest. "I never asked you to pretend. I asked you to be present. I asked you to enjoy the daughter we had, the life we built, but you thought it was a prison."

"It was!" he screams. "Pretending to love you every single day when really you just caught me."

"Caught you?"

"Yeah." He steps back from her finger. "Everybody knows you got pregnant on purpose to trap me. There was no way you were going to let me walk away from you."

Rowan's body is stiff as she squares up to him. "I got pregnant on purpose? You're the one who refused to wear a condom, even though I asked you to."

"You were on birth control," Tommie says in a duh voice. "If you would've known how to use it, none of this would have happened."

I can't hold it in any longer. "Are you for real? You're a fucking EMT and you should know about the success rates of birth control, even when used correctly. They aren't one hundred percent. You're a piece of shit, you know that, right?"

"You don't know me." He throws a glare in my direction.

"I know all I need to know. You've spent years letting Rowan take the blame for something that's your fault. Who goes inside to get a beer, leaving their four-year-old by themselves, near a pool? I'll tell you who does that - a sick fuck who's only concern is themselves."

"She forgot about me." He looks at Rowan like he wants to kill her. It takes everything I have not to step in front of her and take the laser-focused glare. "As soon as we had Etta, I was gum on the bottom of her shoe, everything was about Etta. There wasn't enough left of her for me."

There's a quietness between the three of us and then I

hear Rowan speaking again. "I was a teenager, a new mother, a new wife, and I was taking certification courses. I don't know what else I could have done differently to make you feel like you were my priority, but she was my top. She was counting on us to take care of her, Tommie. She needed us to change her diapers, give her food, shelter, love, and everything in between. We weren't the most important people in our lives anymore, and I'm sorry if you felt like I abandoned you, but you abandoned me."

"Whatever," he scoffs.

"No, you did. My parents had to come get me from the psychward. They had to deal with all the damn therapy I went through. You didn't even file for divorce, you left me there in goddamn limbo. You're the worst person I've ever known," she spits out. "The absolute worst because in the end, you didn't love me. There was no way you could have."

"I resented you," he spits out the word. "And I still do."

"Then why do you want her to call you her husband?" I press the question I've had since he muttered the words.

"She's mine," he answers simply.

"She's not a piece of property to be owned, and fuck you if you think so."

The air is thick with so many unshed emotions between these two, and anger on my part. I'm not sure what's going to happen, but I'm willing to be the bigger man here. To walk away.

Until he opens his mouth again.

"That's okay, she was never a good lay anyway. Which is why I had to cheat on her while we were married. The reason I didn't see Etta? I was FaceTiming with my girlfriend."

I hear her gasp and I feel the anger flowing through my

veins like hot, fucking lava. I don't even have enough time to talk myself out of it, when I hear and feel my fist crack his nose. "You son of a bitch."

"Cutter!" she screams, reaching for my biceps, trying to hold me back.

"You broke my nose!"

"You're lucky I didn't break your dick. How could you do that to her? To your family? You're the worst fucking person I've ever had the displeasure to be in the same space with. You don't deserve her." I wrap my arm around Rowan's neck, pulling her in close. "You had no idea what you had, and I'm glad you lost it, because it allowed me to pick up the pieces of her shattered soul. I might not be the best guy around, but I'm a thousand percent better than you."

I turn, forcing her to come with me.

"Should we help him?" she whispers as she looks back at him.

"Did he help your daughter? Let him choke on his own damn blood. It would serve him right."

We're quiet as we get into her car, and I know immediately I have to ask, I can't go to her apartment without knowing the answer to this question, I need to have her in my life.

"Move to Laurel Springs. Stay with me and build a life with me."

She glances over, her face red, her breath faster than normal. "I want to, but you were about to not trust me when I said he's my ex-husband."

"That's me and my hang-ups, it has nothing to do with you. Notice I corrected myself? Please come home with me, let us build a family together and let me show you what that looks like."

She wants to, her eyes shine bright, and those pink cheeks of hers are full of life.

"Okay."

"Okay?"

"Yeah." A smile spreads across her face. "I'll come live with you."

"This will be the best decision of your life." I grab her up in my arms, hugging her tightly.

"Might be my worst," she teases.

"Never." I kiss her temple, closing my eyes, knowing what a lucky fuck I am.

CHAPTER THIRTY-ONE

Rowan

CUTTER IS GONE, and I'm alone, but I have a plan today. I haven't been over to my parents' for Sunday dinner since we lost Etta. All the things we used to do had tarnished, no longer shining for any of us. Looking at the empty spot where her seat sat was more painful than any of us had ever imagined.

Getting out of my car, I take a deep breath when I realize I'm the last one to show up. Truth be told, even though I called my mom and told her I'd be coming, I don't think any of them truly thought I'd be here. But it's imperative I be here today, I have to explain to them what's going to happen. I don't necessarily need their blessing, but I want it. I desperately need them to understand what I've been going through, and the only way to do that is to tell them. After talking all of these things out with Cutter, I now know how badly I've hurt myself by not speaking about Etta earlier. Weirdly I'd decided by not acknowledging how much losing her affected my life, I was doing better. Being open with Cutter proved to me I wasn't doing better.

My mom opens the door as I walk slowly up the front porch. "I'm so glad you're here, Rowan."

"Me too, Mom." I hug her tightly.

I mean it, and I'm surprised by how much I do.

When I walk in, everyone stops what they're doing, staring at me. "Don't act like you've never seen me before, this isn't the first time I've been to dinner here."

"It's the first time in a long time," my dad grunts from where he sits at the head of the table.

I knew he was going to be the hardest of them, and even though I expected it, it hurts slightly. Walking behind him, I put my arm around him and kiss his head. "Love you too, Dad."

He grunts, and I grin. Things will be fine with him, I know they will be. Having a seat between Sullivan and Braylon, I grasp hands with them as we bow our heads to pray.

Closing my eyes, I'm taken back to another time. In some ways it's almost like I never left, in others it's like I was never here to begin with. Dad finishes grace and we all lift our heads up, muttering Amen.

Now, to figure out the best time to explain to my family what I'm going to do.

The time comes a lot sooner than I expect it to when Braylon opens his mouth. "Heard you've been spending time with the EMT from Laurel Springs."

I nod, before wiping my mouth with my mother's good cloth napkins. Those being here, more than anything, shows how happy she is that I've showed up. "I had hoped to ease you into this." I give Braylon a look of irritation. He and I have always been the two at each other's throats. Call it middle and youngest child syndrome. "But since he's mentioned it, I figure I might as well be honest with my intentions in the next few weeks."

The only one not looking at me with the expectation I'm about to tell them I'm having another nervous breakdown is Sullivan. "I'm moving to Laurel Springs."

Closing my eyes, I wait.

For what I'm not sure, but when I thought about this, it played out so clearly in my mind. My dad would yell, my mom would cry, Braylon would tell me I'm an idiot and berate me for how stupid I am to be moving in with a man I've only known for a short time.

But none of that happens.

"Is everyone okay?" I ask, opening one of my eyes slightly.

I figure I may have to dodge a few thrown objects, but again I'm surprised.

The first person to have any reaction is my dad. He clears his throat, before he takes a drink of his sweet tea, and then looks me dead in the eye.

It's the stare he's used to get more than one criminal to confess, and I'm nervous he's using it on me right now.

"Is this what you want? Does he make you happy?"

I mull the questions over in my head, trying to figure out the best way to answer them. It's then I realize the only way I can answer them is to be honest.

"Yes, this is what I want, and he makes me happier than I've been since I lost Etta."

The group is still quiet and this father of mine, who usually says nothing at all clears his throat again. "I think it's time you do what makes you happy, Ro. Everyone had a preconceived notion about how you should have reacted when you lost Etta. We all kind of expected you to pick up where you left off and just continue on. When you had your breakdown, we didn't know how to deal. We should have gone to counseling with you."

"I wanted you to," I butt in. I asked them more than once if they'd go with me, but none of them ever said yes. Now I'm mature enough and far enough away from it that I can see they didn't want to go because they would have had to open themselves up so wide, but back then it was a slap in the face.

"It wasn't about you," Braylon argues. "It was about us and not being able to come to grips with what happened. Not only could we not save Etta, but we couldn't save you from yourself and your memories."

"I took most of the blame," Dad speaks quietly. "I was the one who said you should get married because you were pregnant. I believed it was the right thing to do. Looking back now, I know I pressured you in ways I never should have."

"I could have said no," I whisper.

"No you couldn't have," Mom continues. "We thought that was the right thing to do so we would have made sure you did it. None of us realized what your life with Tommie was going to be like. No one knew we didn't have forever with Etta, and that's what I hate the most. You won't get to see her grow up and blossom into the type of young woman you are."

Tears are silently streaming down my face. I needed this, to talk to them before I left, to purge everything and start over. There's no way I can start a new life if I'm still hanging on to all these memories and bad feelings.

"Can you just promise me that you'll let me make my

own decisions from now on? You'll trust that even if I don't have experience, I do know myself."

Dad grins over at me. "You've turned into a fine woman, Ro. You know your mind, you know what you want, and you go after it. You don't stop until you get it. There's nothing more I can ask for my kids. I'm proud of you."

"Even if I'm not a boy?"

I push out the fear I've had for so very long. That I would never measure up to my brothers in his eyes.

"Even if you aren't a boy. Believe it or not, I'm more proud of you because you've never taken the easy way out and you've never gotten by on the power of your last name." He looks pointedly at my brothers.

"We're gonna miss you." Mom comes over and hugs me. "But I think this is a good move for you. You get away from the memories, and make new ones."

"Thanks." I smile through the tears. "New memories is exactly what I need."

"So, uh..." Sully clears his throat. "About Laurel Springs..."

CHAPTER THIRTY-TWO

Cutter

I'M off work early today, and I find myself driving by The Café. Mom's car is parked in its normal spot, and Dad's truck is parked next to hers. Since they're both here, I decide to stop. I've never been the type of person to need approval from my parents. That's more up Ransom's alley, but again I made them live with me dropping out of school and losing my scholarship. I never told them exactly what happened either, always too embarrassed to put voice to the situation.

Today though, I decide if I'm going to start a new life with Rowan, I need to have a clean slate, including with my parents.

When I walk in, there aren't many people inside, the lunch rush is long past, and that's probably why Dad's decided to come visit. Mom usually uses the downtime to make orders and do anything else that doesn't get completed in the morning.

Because I know my parents, I make sure and knock loudly on her office door. I don't just barge in. Been there, done that, and have the therapy bills to prove it.

"Come in."

Since she said come in, they must at least be clothed. When I walk in, they both look up at me, surprise on their faces.

"What do I owe this pleasure?" Mom asks, coming around the desk to hug me tightly.

"Was just driving through." I lift her slightly off the ground with the strength of my hug. "Saw both your cars parked here and thought I'd stop in."

Dad knows me better than anyone, he looks at me like he can see right through me. "What do you need to talk about?" He asks, before I even have a seat.

"Maybe he just wants to come say 'hi' to us," Mom gripes to him. "Why do our kids always have to have an ulterior motive when they stop by to say hi? You're going to make it so that they never come by anymore."

They begin to argue slightly, if you can even call it that, but before they get too far into it, I put my hand up, stopping them. "Dad's right, I do have some stuff I want to talk to you about."

"See." Dad raises an eyebrow, giving her a look of triumph.

"Oh stuff it, Holden."

"I'll stuff it…"

"No, no more!' I yell. "Please no more. Can you two just let me talk?"

They stop their arguing, playful as it may be, and give me their full attention. "There's just a few things I have to get off my chest. I've needed to do it for a while, and since I'm going to be starting a new phase of my life soon, I'd like to start it without this hanging over me."

It's apparent they quickly realize I'm serious.

"Go on." Mom reaches out to put her hand over mine.

"When I came back here from Tuscaloosa, I was broken, upset, and not sure how the rest of my life was going to go. I'd been hurt in ways I couldn't express. The only reason Ransom knew was because he was there that day. He saw what happened, and I begged him not to tell anyone else."

"Ransom's a good brother," Dad says. "Every time I've asked him, he's told me to ask you."

"Why haven't you?"

My dad, who always has an answer for everything, is silent.

"I wanted you to ask me, I wanted to be able to confide in you, but I couldn't bring myself to tell you what had happened. Then everyone heard about me losing my scholarship and it turned into I was a fuck-up who didn't know how to take care of the things he was given. But neither one of you asked me what happened. That hurt more than anything."

Their faces are sober as they realize what I've said is true.

Mom is the first to speak. "I thought I was respecting your space. You were an adult who was living his own life. You'd told me that enough times." She shrugs. "I had so many secrets when I was your age, and I had my reasons for keeping them, I thought you were doing the same."

"But I wasn't," I finish for her.

"I'm sorry," she apologizes. "So sorry you expected more from us and we let you down."

"My dad and I," Dad starts, "we never had those

father/son talks like I have with y'all. It's hard for me, still hard for me to sit down and get all up in my feelings with you two. Y'all were raised in such a different way than me. When you didn't want to talk about what happened, I didn't ask because I didn't want to face the fact you'd lost something so precious. I felt like a failure as a parent. Felt like I didn't teach you how to appreciate things in life. It was easier for me to believe you were a screw-up, and if you tell me I'm wrong, then I'm wrong and I apologize from the depths of my soul. But you were an adult and I wanted to believe you were handling things the way you needed to."

"I want to tell you what happened." I look at the two of them. "If you're willing to hear me out."

"I think I speak for both of us" - Mom moves her chair around her desk - "when I say we're ready to listen."

So I launch into the whole sordid tale and let them know I lost my scholarship because I fell in love with the wrong girl.

"I beat the shit out of that guy, and it was either I leave, or he press charges and then the NCAA find out the football program had recruiting violations," I finish. "Then I would have had to admit I'd unknowingly taken bribes. Neither one of those things was a good look for me."

"Why didn't you tell me?" Dad looks pissed. "I could have helped you."

"Exactly the reason you didn't ask what was going on. I was an adult who needed to take care of his own shit. And that's what I did. I mapped out a plan to get my EMT certification, figured out how to get a job in Laurel Springs, and went about putting my life back together."

"That couldn't have been easy. I saw you struggling." Mom wipes at tears under eyes. "But I didn't offer to help."

"Because I'd pushed you away so many times in my youth. Look, I know I'm not perfect. I'm never going to be. I know I've fucked up plenty of times and I've lost so many chances, but here's the thing, I don't want to lose those chances anymore. I'm holding on tightly with everything I have."

"Does this have anything to do with Rowan?" Dad asks, his brow raised.

"She's moving up here."

They both look pleased. "Is there anything you need for us to do?" Mom asks. "Dinner a few nights, moving? Whatever you need we'll be here to help. You know we will. We won't let you down, Cutter."

"You've never really let me down," I argue.

Dad gets up walking over to where I'm sitting. He has a seat next to me and puts his arm around my shoulder. "I beg to differ. You just sat here and told me all the ways I've failed you. I'm not gonna fail you again."

"It was once," I remind him. "Once in my entire life. Looking back on it, it doesn't even seem to be that significant."

"The problem is I failed you, no matter how significant or insignificant it was. I promise to be here for you from now on, and if I'm not understanding, hit me over the head and force me to look. Sometimes I don't catch hints."

Mom snickers. "That's the understatement of the year.

"I gotta go start getting the place ready for Rowan. She's moving in later this week. I just wanted to stop and clear the air. I don't want all this hanging over me, especially not when I'm trying to be the bigger person."

"That was mature of you." Dad grins.

"You'll make a man out of me yet," I laugh.

"You've already made a man out of yourself."

That may very well be the best compliment anyone has ever given me.

CHAPTER THIRTY-THREE

Rowan

"YOU DON'T HAVE to be so sad," I tease Isaac as I reach over, grabbing his hand in mine. "I might not be here after tonight, but we'll still be friends. You can call, text, FaceTime, come visit us - whatever you want to do. Just because I'm moving doesn't mean you're completely out of my life."

"Just never thought you'd leave." He looks over at me, a sad smile on his face.

"I never thought I'd leave either, but it's going to be good for me."

The more I say it the more I believe it. Maybe things had to happen the way they have for me to be able to appreciate it.

"You're gonna miss the ocean."

"I will, and I'll miss Shucker's, and my parents, but I have to do something for myself. I've lived so much of my life being that person who was Etta's mom that I didn't know who I was anymore," I say, doing my best to explain it to him.

"No, I get it. I really do, I'm just going to miss you like crazy."

"I'm gonna miss you too. I've never had a friend like you, never had a partner like you and probably never will again. Trust me when I say, I know what I'm going to be missing when I move. It won't be easy, but it's necessary."

"What if they stick me with someone I hate?" he continues.

"Stop being a whiney ass. You'll learn to love them, just like you learned to love me."

"But it took time, Ro. Like we had to come to an understanding. I feel like we just got in our groove and now you're leaving me."

Truth is, I'm sad to be leaving him. Isaac has been the kind of friend to me I needed in my time in despair. Not many would have stuck by me the way he has.

"Well, if you're completely worried about me leaving, you can help me move tomorrow. I happen to know you're off."

He grimaces. "Why would I want to spend my day off helping you move?"

"Because you love me, Isaac, and I would do the same for you."

He pretends to think about it, but I know he's going to help me, otherwise I wouldn't have asked him.

"Fuck, okay. Guess I better get used to the layout of Laurel Springs since it looks like I'll be visiting."

"You'll love it."

"Yeah, yeah, yeah."

Cutter

I'M lucky to have the people I do in my life. They've taken both Rowan and Sullivan under their wings, and they've taken it upon themselves to get both of them moved in without complaining.

Ransom lifts the ends of a bed, grunting with the exertion. "God, I'm going to be toast tomorrow, and it's supposed to be arm day."

"Make it rest day," I grit through my teeth as we move down the U-Haul and then back up into the apartment Sullivan is renting.

"Might make it call-in-sick-to-work day."

We laugh, because I know he won't, not unless he can get Stella to stick around with him.

"Da Da Da!" Keegan yells from where he sits over to the side with the girls.

"He's cheering you on, babe," Stella laughs.

"I'm gonna need him to shoot up about three feet, gain some muscles, and come help us," he complains as we continue up the stairs to the open door of the apartment.

They laugh at the two of us as Ransom yells, "Pivot!"

"Laugh all you want. If we ever move again." I look over at Rowan - "You're doing the heavy lifting."

"We'll see about that." She gives me a look that tells me if I'm up for it, tonight she'll show me exactly how much she appreciates the work I'm doing.

"How many more trips do we have?" Ryan asks, as he passes us going the other way.

"Too goddamn many," Ransom complains.

"Dude, what is wrong with you? Who pissed in your cheerios?"

"That child of mine." He looks down at Keegan. "Cockblocked me again."

Normally I'd commiserate with him and be his sounding board, but instead I point down to where he's sitting with Rowan.

"While you're griping about your son being here, that one is wishing her daughter was."

"Damn man, I..." He doesn't say anything, but he wipes his face. "Give me a few minutes."

I watch as my brother goes down the stairs, grabbing his son up, hugging him tightly, kissing him on the cheek, and right then I realize how important she's going to be to this family.

Rowan

CUTTER and I wave at the backs of the group who came to help us today, including the group who helped my brother. Somehow, we got everything moved in one day, and while I'm tired, I'm also wired. With this being my first night in the house with Cutter, I kind of have an idea.

"I'm beat." He yawns as he stretches his arms above his head.

We both took showers while food was being delivered, so we're both as clean as we're going to get. I fake a yawn right along with him. "Me too."

"Let's get locked up and head to bed."

There's a grin on my face as I follow him into the bedroom, eyeing the floor-length mirror he has over to the left-hand side.

"Who gave you that mirror?" I ask again, even though he told me earlier today where he'd gotten it.

"Mom says it's some sort of antique and it's supposed to

make the room look bigger. I have no idea, it's just nice to see if what I've been doing in the gym is working."

He's standing in front of it now, rubbing his stomach.

I go up behind him as close as I dare. When it's obvious he's paying more attention to what's in the mirror than what's around him, I slowly wrap my arms around his stomach.

"Love you too," he chuckles patting my hand with his.

Keeping my arms around his waist, I pull him back slightly, making sure my calves touch the bed, before I slip my hand inside the waistband of his shorts, gripping his cock.

"Ro, what the fuck? Oh my God," he groans, tilting his head back.

Now that his head is tilted back I can speak in his ear. "Let me thank you for letting me come stay with you."

Running my palm over his head, I gather up the moisture leaking from the tip and use it to move down his cock. "You don't have to," he groans when I make the trip again. "You don't have to thank me."

"But maybe I want to, and maybe I want to show you exactly how you make me feel. Just enjoy it."

He swallows so hard I can hear it in the room. "Okay."

It takes me a few minutes, but I coax him down on the floor. I sit behind him, my head off to the side so I can look at what I'm doing in the mirror. "Let's get these off you." I point to the shorts, knowing he's not wearing anything underneath them.

He lifts up so that I can take them off, and that's when I slowly start to stroke his cock, up and down. "Look." I tip my chin to the mirror. "Watch me."

His breath comes quicker, his chest panting with the

shallow inhales and exhales. "That's fucking sexy," he says slowly and quietly.

"You know what else is?"

"What?"

"You trying to hold back." I reach up, putting my hand over his mouth. "Don't scream, Cutter. If I hear you, I stop."

Our eyes meet and he makes a sound deep in his chest. I stop completely, letting go of his cock, watching as it jumps on its own, flexing with the need to be stroked.

"Damnit, Rowan. Put your hand back on me."

"Promise you'll be quiet."

"I can't." His voice is tortured.

"You need to." I quirk a brow at him.

"Okay, I'll be quiet, just please stroke me."

I do ask he asks, putting one hand back over his mouth, the other over his cock, jacking it up and down as his hips start to move.

His hands leave where they've been resting on his thighs to come to his nipples, tweaking them as his eyes move up and down with the motion of my hand. Judging by the hardness of his length, this isn't going to last long, and. As I have the thought, he stiffens, and shoots all over my hand, and his stomach.

"Fucking hell," he pushes the words out in between the pants.

But he's still hard, and I'm hornier than I've ever been.

We look at each other, before he scoots across the carpet, reaching into the drawer beside the bed. I watch with appreciation as he takes a condom out and puts it over his length, getting undressed in record time.

When he lays back on the floor, I get on top and push down.

"Fuck, you're wet, didn't even have to prepare you," he moans as I start to ride him.

"Something about you being so manly all day and taking charge of every situation. You made sure things got done and nobody questioned your authority."

"Baby, if that's what you need, I'll do it for you every day."

Pressing against his chest, I ride him hard and fast, until I feel my body begin to tighten.

"Come for me," he breathes out, his hands moving my hips up and down his body.

I close my eyes, tilt my head back and fly to heaven as he grabs my tits and empties himself into the condom for a second time.

As we come down, we look at each other, giggling, not believing what just happened. When he speaks, it's the best words I've ever heard.

"Welcome home, Ro."

Home.

I'm home.

EPILOGUE

Rowan

LSERT FRIENDSMAS

The past few months have passed like the so much of life does. Some days drag and we're dying for the next one to start, but then we look up and we don't know where they've gone.

Since I moved to Laurel Springs most of my days have been those fast ones, especially where Cutter and the rest of our friends are concerned. They took me in as one of their own quickly, and I'm not sure I'll ever be able to thank them enough.

But there is something that everybody is looking forward to, and that's the gift exchange.

Whitney got my name, and I got hers.

"If there's not a chick fight after these presents are opened, Imma be pissed," Devante laughs as he looks between the two of us.

He's come into our friend group too, and become my

new partner. We have a lot of fun during our shifts and I wouldn't trade him for anything.

"My money's on Whit," Ryan says from where he sits, nursing his beer.

"Nope, you ain't seen Ro restrain a drug addict trying to get off her stretcher. My girl Ro is takin' her down."

Whitney and I laugh as the group continues to trash talk.

"What do you say?" Sullivan looks up at Cutter.

"I have no dog in this fight. She knows I've always got her back." He tilts his chin at me, giving me a grin I've become very accustomed to.

"Should we open together?" I ask looking at Whitney.

"Sure."

Together we rip open our gifts, each holding up t-shirts and then laughing as we see what they say. The one I gave her says #1 Auburn Fan and the one she gave me says #1 Alabama Fan.

"This is perfect," Ruby laughs. "I need you two to come stand over here next to the tree so I can take a picture."

The two of us are standing, smiling brightly when the flash goes off. "Damn, Ruby, that thing can be seen in outer space."

I close my eyes and then open them, trying to get the dots out of my vision. When I look over to say something to Whitney, she's no longer there. Cutter is, and holy hell he's down on one knee.

"Cutter?"

"Yeah?" He grins.

"Is this what I think it is?"

We've talked about it. Maybe getting married. Even though I've done it once, it wasn't right, nothing about it was what it should have been. I've mentioned I'd be willing to try it with him.

"If you want it, if you want me, and my crazy ass group of friends and family, I want you."

"We want you," Holden says from where he stands behind Leigh, holding her hand.

"Aunt Ro!"

That comes from Keegan, and I dissolve into tears, looking down at Cutter.

"Will you marry me?" he asks, bringing his bottom lip between his teeth. I can't believe he's nervous that I'll say no.

"Yes!" I fall down to the ground, taking him in my arms.

In a flurry of hugs, kisses, well-wishes, and everything in between, he puts the ring on my finger, and I get a moment alone with Sullivan.

"He asked me, you know."

"Did he?"

"Yeah, he asked Dad too, but he asked me, and I told him I can't think of a better man for my sister. He's everything you deserve, Ro. Don't let him go."

"I won't." I reach in, hugging him tightly. "Are you going to look at Christmas lights with us?"

We're heading out as a group in a few minutes to look at all the decorated houses.

"Nah, I'm gonna get Shelby home." He points to the lawyer. "She's had a little too much to drink."

Judging by her red face and bright eyes, Sullivan's right.

"Be safe," I tell him, hugging him again.

"You too."

As we all head in our own directions, I hop into the bed of Ransom's truck, sitting next to Cutter, wrapped up to keep the cold air from getting to my skin. We have a group of vehicles ten deep, as we slowly make our way through the neighborhoods.

Sometime during all this, Keegan comes over and sits with me, and when I look down, he's asleep, curled up in my lap.

Cutter kisses me on the forehead before looking down at his nephew. "We'll have this one day, Ro. I promise you."

I smile, kissing him on the cheek. "I know."

And I do, because after everything I've been through, I finally found my fairytale. They aren't always easy, but they're definitely worth it.

Preorder Book 5 in the LSERT Series - Sullivan

ABOUT THE AUTHOR

Laramie Briscoe is the USA Today and Wall Street Journal Bestselling Author of over 30 books.

Since self-publishing her first book in May of 2013, Laramie has appeared on the Top 100 Bestselling E-books Lists on Amazon Kindle, Apple Books, Barnes & Noble, and Kobo. Her books have been known to make readers laugh and cry. They are guaranteed to be emotional, steamy reads.

When she's not writing alpha males who seriously love their women, she loves spending time with friends, reading, and marathoning shows on Netflix. Married to her high school sweetheart, Laramie lives in Bowling Green, KY with her husband (the Travel Coordinator) and a sometimes crazy cat named Beau.

facebook.com/authorlaramiebriscoe
twitter.com/laramiebriscoe
instagram.com/laramie_briscoe
bookbub.com/authors/laramie-briscoe

REPORT ERRORS/REVIEWS

LEAVE A REVIEW

IF THERE WAS a part you loved of "Tank", please don't hesitate to leave a review and let other readers know!

If you do leave a review, please email me with the link so that I can say a personal 'thank you'!!! They mean a lot, and I want to let you know I appreciate you taking the time out of your day!

Email Me

REPORT AN ERROR

Also, if you find an error, know that it has slipped through no less than four sets of eyes, and it is a mistake. Please let me know, if you find one, and if I agree it's an error. It will be changed. Thank you!

Report Errors

CONNECT WITH LARAMIE

Patreon:
patreon.com/laramiebriscoe
Website:
www.laramiebriscoe.net
Facebook:
facebook.com/AuthorLaramieBriscoe
Twitter:
twitter.com/LaramieBriscoe
Pinterest:
pinterest.com/laramiebriscoe
Instagram:
instagram.com/laramie_briscoe
Mailing List:
http://sitel.ink/LBList
Email:
laramie@laramiebriscoe.com

ALSO BY LARAMIE BRISCOE

Heaven Hill Shorts

Caelin

Christine

Justice

Harley

Jagger

Charity

Liam

Drew

Dalton

Mandy

Rockin' Country Series

Only The Beginning

One Day at A Time

The Price of Love

Full Circle

Hard To Love

Reaper's Girl

The Nashvegas Trilogy

Power Couple

The Moonshine Task Force Series

Renegade

Tank

Havoc

Ace

Menace

Cruise

Laurel Springs Emergency Response Team

Ransom

Suppression

Enigma

Cutter

The MVP Duet

On the DL

MVP

The Midnight Cove Series

Inflame

Stand Alones

Sketch

Sass

Trick

Room 143

2018 Laramie Briscoe Compilation

2019 Laramie Briscoe Compilation

Made in the USA
Columbia, SC
25 June 2020

12266381R00152